A DANCER FROM THE ABBEY

They climbed the stony track.
(*See Chapter 20*)

A DANCER FROM
THE ABBEY

by

ELSIE J. OXENHAM

COLLINS
LONDON AND GLASGOW

First printed in this Edition 1956
Reprinted   1956

PRINTED AND MADE IN GREAT BRITAIN BY
WM. COLLINS SONS AND CO. LTD.
LONDON AND GLASGOW

To
DORIS ACLAND
with love
and all very best wishes,
from
ELSIE JEANETTE OXENHAM

CONTENTS

CHAP.		PAGE
1.	DAMARIS WITH A DIRTY FACE	9
2.	JEN IS LONELY	17
3.	MOTHER OF EIGHT	25
4.	WELCOME FOR BRIAN	33
5.	A FRIEND FOR ROSEMARY	39
6.	A KEY FOR RACHEL	48
7.	NIGHT IN THE ABBEY	54
8.	MARY SPEAKS	61
9.	BRIAN SUGGESTS A HOLIDAY	69
10.	RODDY'S PLACE IN THE FAMILY	76
11.	"MY LADY'S LITTLE BROTHER"	88
12.	CRICKET AT THE MANOR	94
13.	WHAT MISS NIGGER FOUND	103
14.	A TREASURE FOR THE ABBEY	111
15.	AMBROSE AGAIN	117
16.	HELP FOR DAMARIS	123
17.	A MUSICAL EVENING	131
18.	SISTER RACHEL	140
19.	DAMARIS SURRENDERS	151
20.	PICNIC FOR RACHEL	159
21.	A RING FOR DAMARIS	165

CONTENTS

CHAP.   PAGE
22. BRIAN'S GARDEN   172
23. A BADGE FOR BENEDICTA   179
24. A SURPRISE FOR MYONIE   189
25. SEARCH FOR A QUEEN   199
26. CONSULTING THE ABBOT   206
27. A CROWN FOR TESSA   216
28. A RING FOR RACHEL   225
29. HEATHER AND CROCUS   232
30. THE RETURN OF MARY DAMAYRIS   240
31. PLANS FOR A WEDDING   248

CHAPTER I

DAMARIS WITH A DIRTY FACE

"ARE YOU my little Pirouette?" The man jumped
from his car and addressed the girl who sat on
the low wall of the Abbey garden.

"I shouldn't think so," she retorted. "I've never
been called a pirouette. What makes you think I
might be yours?"

"I don't think so, now." He was looking at her
carefully. "No, I'm sure you're not. Where is
she?"

He had been told to look for a girl with a riot
of yellow curls. This girl's hair was so fair as
to be almost white—lint-white; and it curled
demurely and very neatly round her neck. She
wore a smock of khaki-coloured linen, with
breeches showing below, and a soft hat lay on her
knee.

"It sounds to me as if you want Mary Damayris,"
she remarked. "I'm merely Benedicta."

"Benedicta is a good introduction to an Abbey!
Weren't strangers always welcomed with a
blessing?"

"I believe they were. I shall have to sit here
for ever." Benedicta's eyes gleamed.

"To bless strangers," he agreed. "Perhaps you

could begin with me. I do want to see Mary Damayris. Is she here?"

"She's in that corner, making a bonfire. This is her garden; she made it. I'm her assistant."

The visitor's eyes roved over the flowery stretch that lay round the old gate-house and reached to the Abbey walls. "Made it, did she? She's done a good spot of work. You aren't assisting very hard at the moment, are you?"

"I'm tired. We're all tired to-day," Benedicta said, with dignity. "We went to a Coronation last night. The new Queen—May-Queen, at her school—lives here and we went to see her crowned. She's Queen Lavender."

"Most suitable, if she lives in a garden," he responded. "But perhaps you mean she lives in this Abbey?"

"No, at the Hall. The Abbey is in the garden of the Hall. She's really Lady Rosalind Kane, but we forget all that. She'll be called Lavender now."

He raised his brows. "And watching her crowned exhausted you and Mary Damayris?"

"It was more than that. When we came home we talked and were all rather excited. I don't think any of us slept much. If we hadn't talked you wouldn't be allowed to ask about Mary Damayris," Benedicta remarked.

"That's a cryptic saying! May I ask why?"

"Because she wouldn't talk about her dancing. Strangers weren't supposed to know she had ever been Mary Damayris. She was Damaris

Ellerton, or just good old Damson, the Abbey Gardener."

"I'm coming in to talk to you," he announced, and went along by the wall and entered the garden by the gate.

Benedicta sat waiting for him. "Who are you?" she asked. "Did you know Damaris in town? No, you can't have done, for you mistook me for her. But you know about her and you came to find her?"

"I'm Brian Grandison. My dad wrote the music for some of her ballets. I've been in South Africa for seven years, and though, of course, I have come home to see my people at times, I never happened to see Mary Damayris dance. I heard of the accident that broke her career and of her disappearance to live in the country, and I've met some of her former friends, since I came back to London. I want to meet her, even if I can never see her dance. I was greatly moved by the story of her wild leap to save her friend, which ruined her own life. So I came to look her up."

"I see." Benedicta gazed at him with interest. "It's a good thing you didn't come yesterday. She didn't want to talk about those times. But everything's different to-day."

"Another mysterious remark! Won't you explain?"

"She's going back, to be a dancer again," Benedicta said simply. "That's what she told us last night. That's why we talked, and why we couldn't sleep."

"So!" He stood looking down at her. "But I thought she couldn't dance?"

"She found yesterday that she could get the position she'd found impossible; in her hip, you know. She'd been trying for months, but she couldn't do it. Yesterday things came right, and she knows she'll be able to dance again."

"That's marvellous news!" He drew a long breath. "I'd like to congratulate her. May I tell her friends in town? They'll be overjoyed."

"She may let you tell them. It will take a long time; she expects to need all sorts of treatment and then heaps of exercises and practice. It won't come back all at once. But she's sure now she will be able to dance as well as ever."

"I don't wonder you didn't sleep! It must have been a very great moment when she told you."

"And after the crowning and the country dancing! It was midnight when I went home; my landlady wasn't a bit pleased."

" Don't you live here, then?"

" No, I put up in the village. Ray and Dammy haven't room for me in the Abbey."

"Ray and Dammy?" he asked doubtfully.

"Rachel and Damaris. Rachel is Damson's sister, and she takes care of the Abbey; she'll show you round. She's the Abbot."

"I begin to understand," he smiled. "We seem to have begun at the end, but things are coming clear. Do you think I could see our little dancer and give her my congratulations and good wishes?"

"I'll call her. I say, you know, it's not quite fair; she can't help being in a frightful mess. Bonfires always make one dirty. She'll want to clean off the smuts."

"Ask her to forgive me. Tell her I don't mind smuts in the least."

Benedicta grinned. "No, but Mary Damayris may mind—if she thinks about it. Come and look at our garden! The rockeries are called Wirral and Windermere; those are where the stones came from. Don't you like our hyacinths? We're rather proud of them."

Beside the red-rocked Wirral she paused and shouted towards the column of smoke rising in a corner, behind a privet hedge. "Damson! Mary Damayris! You're wanted!"

"Who wants me?" A slim figure appeared at a gap in the hedge, wearing khaki shorts and a green pullover, her hair covered with a green scarf, wound round her head and tied at the back, with the ends hanging over her shoulder. Her hands were dirty and there were undeniable smuts on her cheeks, where she had drawn her fingers across her face.

"He calls you his little something-or-other; pirouette, I think it was."

"What's that?" There was a sudden sharp note in the gardener's voice. "That was what Bernard called me—my dancing partner, you know. I made an ass of myself, putting in extra pirouettes, and Bernard never stopped teasing me. He can't be here, surely?"

"No, it's someone else. He'd heard you called the little pirouette."

"Please forgive me, Miss Damayris." Brian Grandison came forward. "I had no right to use Bernard's name for you. Somehow it just happened."

"He thought I was you, at first," Benedicta remarked. "He's decided now that I'm the Abbey Blessing and I'm to sit for ever at the gate, blessing people as they come in."

"Oh, no, you're not! You're going to weed that tulip bed," Damaris retorted. "There's no time for sitting at gates. But first you can take on this job and damp down my fire. Don't let it get out of hand! We don't want to burn the ilex trees." She pushed back a strand of yellow hair, adding another smudge to her cheek.

"You'd better wash before you talk to anybody," Benedicta said. "You don't look exactly beautiful."

"I wasn't expecting visitors." Damaris glanced at the tall guest defiantly. "Will you see me with a dirty face or will you wait while I go and clean up? Have you ever made a bonfire?"

"Several," he laughed. "If I really may choose I'll do both. I don't want you to go away, but I was told to look for a girl with a lot of curls, and I don't suppose——"

"Oh, you can see them!" Damaris whipped off the scarf and shook her hair loose about her face in a yellow shower. "Is that better? Who are you? You seem to know Martin Bernard?"

"I'm Brian Grandison," and he repeated the

explanation he had given to Benedicta, his eyes gazing at her in delight.

"I've heard of you," Damaris announced. "I've had tea with your people and they talked about you. You gave up a valuable art scholarship, to take your sister to South Africa, because she was ill and couldn't live in England, and your dad and mother didn't want to leave London. You took on the job and gave up your hopes of a career, and stood by your sister. I thought it was a frightfully noble deed."

"They needn't have said anything about that," he protested. "What else could I do? Someone had to go, and Dad's place is in town."

"All the same, it was rather marvellous of you. What happened? Did your sister die?"

"No, she recovered." He smiled down at her. "She's well, so long as she lives out there. She's married. So I've come home, to pick up threads and find a job."

"Oh, good! Will you be able to have the scholarship and go on studying?"

"No, that's ended. I shall do something else."

"Rather rotten to lose the career you'd set your heart on. They told me how keen you were."

"That's something you know all about, isn't it?" he said quietly.

"Well—yes. But I'm going to have my career, after all. Did Benedicta tell you?"

"She did. May I say how glad I am and how I hope to see you dance? I thought there was no chance of it."

"There wasn't, till yesterday. It will be a long time before I'm ready, but I shall dance again some day." There was an exultant ring in her voice.

He smiled in sympathy. "My hearty congratulations! May I be the bearer of the good news, to my dad, and to Georges Antoine, and to Martin Bernard?"

"You may tell them," Damaris conceded. "They'll know what a long time of preparation I shall need. I wrote to Madame Roskova, my teacher, this morning."

"Do go and wash, Damson!" Benedicta urged, coming from a glance at the fire. "You look simply frightful. Mr. Grandison can help me here. And tell Rachel; he'll want to see the Abbey."

"It's quite a good idea," Damaris mocked. "I know I'm a ghastly object. I'll come back!" she shouted, as she sped towards the Abbey entrance.

Brian Grandison laughed as he watched her go. "How marvellously she runs! Look at that leap over the tulips! She's beautiful!"

"She is," Benedicta agreed. "We're dying to see her dance again. Come and look at the fire!"

CHAPTER II

JEN IS LONELY

"I SAY, RAY!" Damaris dashed into the little
parlour within the Abbey walls. "Such an odd
thing!—Yes, I know I'm filthy. I've come in to
wash; it was the bonfire. Ray, a man's turned
up, and he's Brian Grandison, dear old Granny
Grandison's son, who went to South Africa.
You know the story? Blessing's taking care of
him, till I'm clean again." And she disappeared
into the bathroom.

The girl standing by the table, turning over
some papers with one hand, while she stroked
a purring golden cat gently with the other, was
like her in the dark eyes and firm chin, but her
hair was brown and not so curly. She wore a
long white gown, like a monk's robe, with a
girdle at the waist, her uniform as Guardian of
the Abbey ruins. Her eyes were wistful and
restless, as if she carried a burden.

"John Grant Grandison, the composer—his
son?" she asked. "How odd! What brought him
here?"

"To see me, my dear. I'd have been worried
yesterday, but it's all right to-day," Damaris
shouted joyfully.

Rachel's lips pinched. "I *can't* get used to it," she said to herself. "I'm going to lose her, and—what's that?" she said aloud.

"You know what it is," Damaris called, as the clear high notes of a pipe sounded across the garth. "Go and talk to her! It's Lady Jen; couldn't be anyone else."

Rachel went out to the garth, where tall, curly-haired Jen Marchwood stood at the entrance to the tresaunt, piping a processional morris on a three-hole English pipe, whose notes were like silver bells. Rachel had seen her already this morning, when, very early, she had taken home the small car which had been lent to them for the Coronation jaunt to town; and in a few hurried words she had told the news Damaris had given late the night before.

"Oh, Ray, how splendid!" had been Jen's comment. "I'll hear more about it presently. I must get my family off to school. Tell Dammy-Marry how very, very glad I am. You must be thrilled and happy. It's quite wonderful, after all this time!"

But now, as she came across the garth, her face was sober. "I've come to be cheered up. The Abbey is the place for people to find comfort. I'm definitely lonely, Abbey Lady. What are you going to do about it?"

"Hear about it, I hope. How can you possibly be lonely, with your house full of children and babies, Lady Jen? That jolly tune didn't sound in the least sad."

"That was to keep up my spirits. Kenneth's gone off to town for the day, just when I need him for company. Men don't always understand these things."

" But why this sudden loneliness?" Rachel asked. "I'd laugh, if I didn't think you really mean it."

"I do mean it. The elder boys went off to York yesterday, and to-day my big daughter has gone to school for the first time, and my biggest little boy at home has gone with her to the Kindergarten. I'm missing them terribly, and I'm aching to know how Rosemary's getting on, alone in Wycombe. It's all I can do to keep myself from leaping into the car and rushing down to school to ask if she's all right."

"Oh, you mustn't do that! Think how people would laugh at her!"

"I know. I have to bear it. But I don't know how I can wait till the afternoon."

"Rosemary is almost nine. She should be all right," Rachel said consolingly.

"She's such a quiet little person," Jen explained. "Not in the least like me. And she's been dreading going to school. The one thing that made her go off happily was the thought that she must be there to take care of Mike, who is only six. It was really rather nice, Ray! Rosemary shrank from school, but she couldn't let Mike down, and as he was to start she had to go to look after him."

"How sweet of her!" Rachel laughed. "Oh,

she'll be all right! She's always been motherly to the little ones."

"The joke is that Mike doesn't want to be looked after. He's eager to be a big boy and go to school and be different from the babies. Rosemary will find she isn't needed, but I hope by that time she'll have made friends."

"I'm sure she will. Queen Lavender and Jansy will keep an eye on her. You haven't sent Katharine as well?"

"I couldn't spare Katharine," Jen said definitely. "She's invaluable to me."

"Oh, Lady Jen! At four and a half?"

"Most decidedly. She takes charge of the twins and leaves Nanny to see to Baby."

"She's beginning early! What can she do, at that age?"

"She takes a twin firmly by each hand and marches them off into the garden; they can just toddle as far as that—they're a year and a half old. Katharine plays with them for hours at a time."

"How very helpful! Oh, then, I quite see Mike's point of view. He doesn't want to stay at home with the babies."

"No, he's ready for school. He feels completely grown-up. He asked me yesterday when he could go to York with Andrew and Tony."

"He'll soon be off your hands altogether."

"That's the worst of children. You lose them so quickly; almost as bad as kittens. But Rosemary and Mike are only staying for the half-day

at present. The car is to fetch them after school
dinner; it would be too long for Mike to stay all
day. Shall I come to the Abbey at two o'clock, and
take them out of the car and bring them home
through the garden? The walk would be good for
them, after being indoors all morning. Poor
babes! I'm sorry for them, having to start on
such a lovely day!"

"And we'd hear how Rosemary managed at
school." Rachel grasped the point. "Oh, please,
Lady Jen! I do want to know about her!"

"I'll do it," Jen promised. "What's the matter?"
and her kind eyes scanned Rachel's face keenly.
"Didn't you sleep last night? You look tired.
Was Lavender's crowning too much for you?"

"Not the crowning." Rachel looked back at her
bravely.

"I suppose Damaris worked you up with her
excitement? It's great news! She really thinks
she'll be all right again?"

"She's quite sure. I'm glad; very glad. But—
don't you see, Lady Jen? You generally understand."

"I think I understand now," Jen said gently.
"You feel you're going to lose her. Or the Abbey
—which? I've been wondering what you would
do, ever since you told me."

"That's what we talked about last night."
Rachel caught her breath. "I can't leave the
Abbey; it's my job. Damaris won't let me go
with her; she said it quite definitely. She wants
me to stay here, and I've promised to be happy

about it. But it isn't going to be easy. We've always been together."

"It's my problem with Rosemary over again. You've mothered Damaris; now you have to let her go away and win through alone. Ray dear, I do understand. I know just how you feel. You'll be lonely; there's no help for it. But you must be brave. She's strong enough to stand on her own feet, and Madame Roskova will see that she comes to no harm."

"You do think I'm right to stay here?" Rachel asked wistfully. "I hate to let her go alone, back to that difficult life. She'll be taken care of all right, but she'll want me to talk to; she'll want to tell me everything, and to discuss things with me. But I can't let down the Abbey now!"

"Most certainly you can't. It isn't merely the Abbey, you know. We might find another guide, but you're becoming the counsellor and confidant of all these younger girls. They come to you for advice; we've seen that. You couldn't let down Jansy and Lavender!"

"I'm not good enough," Rachel objected. "I try to help, but I don't always know what to say."

"You seem to manage very well. They all turn to you. Oh, Rachel, don't go away! We're so glad to have you in the Abbey! Joan said so last night."

Rachel coloured. Joan—Mrs. Raymond—was the owner of the Abbey and her employer, and her good opinion meant much to the Abbey Guardian.

Jen slipped a hand through her arm. "We'll be lonely together. We'll buck up one another."

"You said you came to the Abbey to be comforted," Rachel said. "But it seems to me you're doing the comforting."

"You must be careful, you know," Jen said earnestly. "Rosemary hasn't an idea how I feel, but Dammy-Marry knows all about it. Don't spoil her joy in her new future! I'm sure she's radiantly happy. Where is she? I must tell her how glad I am."

"She's getting rid of the smuts from a bonfire." Rachel gave a little laugh. "Someone has come from town to see her and she had a dirty face, so she's cleaning up."

"Who is the unexpected visitor?"

"The son of John Grant Grandison, who wrote the music for her ballets. She hadn't seen him before; he's been abroad."

"A man!" Jen raised her brows. "Mary Damayris must be careful. There's no room for men in her life!"

"She knows that. There'll be plenty of men, but not in the way you mean. I wish there could be just one man; the right man!" Rachel broke out.

"You'd like to see her married?"

"I want her to be happy. I wouldn't mind losing her, if it were for marriage. I don't like letting her go back to a stage life alone."

"Perhaps the right man will come along. But could she care enough for any man to give up her dancing for his sake?" Jen pondered the problem.

"I don't believe she could. Dancing is her whole life."

"She thinks so, anyway. But love can be very compelling, and Mary Damayris is an artist and doesn't take things lightly. It may happen," said Jen hopefully. "I'm glad she can dance again, but I agree with you that marriage would be even happier. Let me have a look at this young Grandison!"

CHAPTER III

MOTHER OF EIGHT

" I SHALL pipe a little tune for him," Jen murmured, as they went towards the garden.

"What's that?" Brian Grandison stamped out the remains of the fire and looked at Benedicta, as the clear high notes came to him across the tulips and hyacinths.

"'Trunkles,' played on an Old English pipe. It has only three holes and it's made of wood. Isn't it pretty?"

"Like a silver bird-note. But how does she do it, with only three holes? Oh, Miss Damayris! I thought you were making that music?"

Damaris came running from the Abbey, but the music went on. His eyes devoured her hungrily, for her curls were brushed and her face was clean, though she still wore her shorts and pullover.

"I'm not the piper! How's my fire? All safe?—oh, good! I guess you'd like to wash now, wouldn't you? Benedicta must show you the bathroom. We really have a bathroom, though it's rather surprising; small, but useful! The piper is Lady Marchwood, from the Manor, next door," she added, seeing his eyes on the two who had just come from the Abbey gateway—

Rachel in her white monk's gown, and tall, fair Jen, piping like a schoolboy.

"She doesn't look like the mother of eight, does she?" Benedicta remarked.

Jen and Rachel were coming along a narrow path, bordered by bushes of lavender, with the first marigolds just opening into flower.

"The mother of—oh, surely not!" Brian exclaimed.

"It's true," Damaris told him. "Two big boys at school in York; the eldest is twelve. A girl and a small boy who have gone to school for the first time to-day. Another small girl, twin boys, and a very new girl, a few weeks old. Quite a respectable family, isn't it?"

"I shouldn't have thought she was more than twenty-five," he marvelled. "Did she begin at fourteen?"

"She's older than she looks," Benedicta grinned. "But she married early, I believe. Lady Jen! We've been telling him you're the mother of eight children. He doesn't believe it; he says you must have had the first when you were fourteen."

"No, twenty," said Lady Marchwood. "I really am an old lady. I'm not going to have any more—at present!" with a mischievous glance at Brian. "I keep a hope that when I'm really old, perhaps forty, I may have one more; a sort of back-ender. But I'm content with our little crowd. I call them our Pieces of Eight—treasure, you know. Have you ever seen a pipe like this, Mr. Grandison?"

"Indeed I haven't. I'm very curious to know

how you can make so many notes from three holes."

"And the open note; it's really four. I can make eleven notes, but the tune has to fit into that range. If it goes beyond the eleven, you have to cheat; I'm quite good at cheating! Held and played with the left hand, you see; the right hand is supposed to play the tabor—a little drum. Are you keen on music like your father?"

"No, it turned to painting with me. I couldn't make anything original in music, but at one time I had an idea I could paint. That was stamped on by circumstances; I sketch a bit, to amuse myself, but I don't turn out anything really worth while. I've been in Africa for seven years, and now I want some sort of job at home."

"Africa? Kenya?" Jen cried. "You must meet my husband. He lived there once and I think he's left part of his heart in Kenya."

"It was Rhodesia, I'm afraid," Brian said. "But I'd like to meet—is it Lord Marchwood?"

"Oh, no, thanks be! He's only a baronet; it's quite bad enough! You must meet Kenneth; he'll love to compare notes with you. But you won't persuade him that Rhodesia can be anything like Kenya. What sort of job are you looking for?"

Brian's eyes swept over the garden. "This!" he said comprehensively. "No, I'm not crazy and it isn't a sudden idea. I want to be instructed about those rock-gardens. My grandmother left me her old house, in the north, and I'm told the rock-garden is rather good; I haven't seen it yet. I've a hunch that I might develop it and do something in the market-garden line, specialising in rock plants. It's near Ambleside, in the Lake District——"

"Ambleside!" There was a united shout from the Ellerton girls.

"It's our home!" Rachel cried. "We come from Grasmere. We've an old farm house on the fells— oh, you don't know me yet! I'm Rachel Ellerton, the Guardian and guide to the Abbey ruins, and Damaris is my little sister."

"A hefty little sister," Damaris grinned. "Mr. Grandison, give our love to the fells, when you go to see your house. I believe you could make something good out of your idea. But it might not pay for some time."

"That wouldn't matter," he said simply. "I want to do a job that will satisfy me and be useful to other people. Granny left me a good deal, because she felt I'd stood by my sister and pulled her through, when no one else could do it. I wouldn't speak of it, but I know you've heard the story."

"You took care of your sister, on behalf of the family," Damaris agreed. "That was very fair of the old lady. I hope you'll have luck with your venture. Gardens are jolly things, when you have to build up a new career." Her eyes sought Jen's, as if to say: "Have you heard? Do you understand?"

"Dammy-Marry, I am so glad for you!" Jen cried. "It's marvellous news, and I wish you all the luck you've just wished Mr. Grandison. You must be very happy to-day."

"I'm going back!" Damaris gave a shout. "I shall dance again! All that wonderful life is going to be mine! Oh, Lady Jen, can you play 'Shepherd's Hey'?"

Jen raised her brows. "I can. But what use is a morris dance to you, my child?"

"Oh, please!" Damaris pleaded.

"Oh, play it for her!" Benedicta cried. "I don't know why, but if she wants it, let her have it!"

"I know why," Rachel said. "Please, Lady Jen!"

"Please, Lady Marchwood!" Brian urged.

"There's no difficulty about 'Shepherd's Hey.' It's a real pipe tune. But I don't understand," Jen protested.

She began to play the jolly lilting melody, and Brian and Benedicta found their feet tapping to the infectious rhythm. Then they forgot everything, for Mary Damayris was dancing on a patch of green lawn, ringed round with scarlet tulips, with all the wild abandon and beauty that had given such joy to thousands.

"It's horribly bad," she cried, as she paused. "But you people won't know that. I can do it, and that's the great thing. I'll soon work up to something decent again."

"Bad!" said Brian. "You're the loveliest moving thing I've ever seen, Mary Damayris."

"Do some more, Damson!" Benedicta pleaded.

"Like it?" Damaris asked casually. "You've teased often enough to see me dance. Satisfied now?"

"No! I want to go on watching you for ever."

"Hear, hear!" cried Brian.

Damaris bobbed. "I can't curtsy in shorts. Thank you, kind lady and gentleman!"

Rachel was explaining to Jen, who was urgently demanding an answer. "Marry always dances when she hears that tune. It came on the radio, when we were in Annecy, seven years ago, and she jumped up and danced, and Papa Berthelot saw her and insisted that she must become a dancer. That started her on her career. The same thing happened at Hikers' Halt, the tea-cottage near Ambleside, and she danced there too. ' Shepherd's Hey ' always sets her off. It's nothing like your morris dance, of course."

"It's very, very different," Jen said solemnly. "But I'm glad to have seen it. It *is* a jolly tune! I don't wonder she can't resist it. But it's the oddest ' Shepherd's Hey ' I ever saw. Mary Damayris, you're as beautiful as you used to be, when you dance. Thank you for the treat! When you're the idol of the London stage again, we'll remember how you danced for us among the tulips."

"Nice of you!" Damaris laughed. "Your music's marvellous, Lady Jen. It's not the same as the radio version; that works up so tremendously at the end. Papa Berthelot loved what I made out of it. But yours is the same tune, without the frills. No, not any more just now, Blessing! But you shall watch me practise, if it won't bore you. I couldn't bear it before, but I shan't mind now. Ray, aren't you going to show Mr. Grandison the Abbey? Lady Jen can talk to Blessing and me."

"But I want to talk to Blessing and you, too," he protested. "I want to be told all about rock-gardens. You're going to instruct me, I hope."

"There's time for both," Jen interposed. "I'm going home to my neglected twins and my little girls; but I'm coming back about two o'clock, to meet Rosemary and Mike on their way from school. Mr. Grandison, I really would like you to meet Kenneth; he'll enjoy a chat with you so much. But he won't be home till seven. Couldn't you come again to-morrow and spend a few days with him? It would give him real pleasure."

"It would give me very great pleasure," Brian said promptly. "It's more than kind of you to suggest it. But are you sure Sir Kenneth——?"

"Certain," Jen assured him. "There's nothing he'd like better. Come to the Manor for lunch at one, and we'll phone him and arrange it. He's lunching at his club, so we can get hold of him there. He always tells me where he'll be at lunch-time, or else he rings me up. These girls can't feed a hungry man, and we don't want you to go to the inn——"

"We could. We'd like to," Rachel began.

"You'll show him the Abbey, and Dammy-

Marry will tell him about her Wirral and
Windermere." Jen spoke with authority. "Send
him to me about one o'clock; Benedicta can show
him the path. There's no one at the Hall, so he
needn't mind trespassing in the garden; Joy and
Mary are having lunch at The Pallant and Ivor's
in town, as usual. Only Nanny and the babies
are at the Hall. Take him in and let him wash,
Abbey Lady; bonfires are messy things. I'll see
you presently, and we'll hear Rosemary's adventures at school. I'm quite sure Mike is having a
joyful time! I wish I could feel as certain that
my daughter is happy. Thank you for your dance,
Mary Damayris! But it was an odd ' Shepherd's
Hey '! Very odd indeed! " and shaking her head
seriously, Jen walked away, piping " Hunting the
Squirrel " as she went.

CHAPTER IV

WELCOME FOR BRIAN

"Come and find our little bathroom, Mr. Grandison," Rachel said. "Then you can have a look at the Abbey; or if other visitors come you can go back to the garden."

"Why does Lady Jen want to see Rosemary and Mike in such a hurry?" Damaris asked, following them.

Benedicta fetched a fork and a trug and knelt to weed the tulip bed. "Too many of them in there, and it's their house. I'll keep in the background. The nice man likes Mary Damayris! He'd better take care. She won't marry anybody. But he's old enough to look after himself; he's not a kid boy. Here's our old friend shepherd's needle, coming up in masses; I must get it out, or Damson will have fits."

Rachel explained Jen's anxiety over her eldest daughter, as she led the way to the Abbey gate. "Rosemary should be all right, with Jansy to look after her and with Lavender as her Queen. They all went together to school in the car with Frost, but Lady Jen is sending Henderson to fetch her babes before afternoon school, as a whole day seems so long for them at first."

"Oh!" said Brian Grandison, as she led him through the gate. "Oh, this is beautiful! May I look?"

The green square of the cloister garth lay before him, walled by old grey buildings, with pointed arches below and a row of long lancet slits above.

Rachel stood aside to let him see. "Up there was the monks' dormitory; each man had a window and a stone seat below it, beside his bed. Under the dormitory is the chapter-house, and the day-room, where they worked. These wide Perpendicular windows are the refectory, a lovely big light hall. You must see it all presently. Oh, thank you, Marry!"

Damaris had darted across the garth and was pulling on two ropes which hung down the refectory wall. A high note sounded, and another, and a low note repeated twice; all that again, and again, and then two high notes and only one low, as a finish.

Rachel laughed. "Those are the old Abbey bells; it's not very long since they were found, after being lost for centuries. The high one, Cecilia, was hidden away at the farm next door; the deep one, Michael, was buried under a fall of cliff, up on the hill. Their names were written on them. We ring them to welcome visitors and on special occasions, and we have a code—the bells always mean something. Damaris rang—' Glad to see you! ' several times, and then ' Welcome home.' A real greeting for you!"

"Well, he has come home, after seven years," Damaris urged.

"A beautiful greeting! I appreciate it very deeply," Brian exclaimed.

"Now come and see where we live, and have that much-needed wash," and Rachel led him through a low doorway. "These rooms are right inside the walls. They used to be the refectory of the lay brothers."

He gazed round in delight at grey walls, rose-pink curtains at long narrow windows, a red-shaded lamp, books in shelves, flowers and pictures everywhere.

The golden cat had been washing himself on the crimson cloth, but he rose at once and came to the edge of the table to meet them.

Rachel pulled his soft ears gently. "He always rises when we come in. He's very polite."

"He's a very fine fellow," Brian said.

"He thinks so! The black person in the chair is a little lady. She isn't quite so courteous! Our pictures may interest you. They're water-colour sketches of the Lake District; our home, as we told you. Here are Grasmere and Rydal Water—Ullswater—Grisedale Tarn—the top of Helvellyn."

"They're only prints," Damaris added. "We don't go in for anything posh like originals."

"They're charming, all the same; a feast of colour, in blue and grey and green and purple," he said. "But these aren't prints?" He bent to look closely at a row of pen and ink sketches, hung below the coloured pictures. "Surely these are drawings of your ruins, originals and very good ones?"

"Right in every particular," Damaris told him proudly. "How clever of you!"

"Those were Christmas presents," Rachel said. "Damaris was given one, a year and a half ago, and it seemed so suitable in here that our friends asked, last Christmas, if we would like some more. We said there was nothing we'd like better, so they told Rob Quellyn to do six, one from each bit of the family. Rob Quellyn is a cousin of Sir Ivor Quellyn, who lives at the Hall; you'll know about him, through your father."

"I haven't met him, but I've heard of him often. And his cousin does these exquisite little drawings?"

"He came to stay at the Hall with his wife and baby boy, after Christmas. He told us to choose our subjects and added another from himself and one from Mrs. Quellyn, because they are both so fond of the Abbey. So we have nine Quellyn sketches, and we're very proud of them."

"These two paintings, of the garth and the gate-house, were given to us long ago," Damaris added.

"It makes an enchanting little home. The old walls are a wonderful background and your pictures give all the colour you need." Brian looked round in approval.

A glance passed between the girls, and Rachel said grimly, "Our aunt was caretaker here for

years, and her choice for the walls was pink.
The lovely old stone was colour-washed pink.
We're still rejoicing in our clean cool grey, after
more than a year. Now here's the bathroom—
green and white, you see. We'll leave you to get
rid of the traces of the bonfire. When you're
ready, you shall see the Abbey, or the garden, as
you wish."

"My room is all green and gold," Damaris
informed him. "And Rachel's work-room is a
lovely blue. Did you know she writes stories?
Well, she does; and gets them printed, too."

"'Curiouser and curiouser,' as Alice would say,"
he quoted. "I really have come to an enchanted
place!"

"You'll think so, when Ray shows you the
Abbey and tells you all the stories," Damaris
retorted. "She does it jolly well."

Rachel closed the bathroom door firmly. "Let
the poor man have his wash and clean-up. I'm
going to make coffee. Fetch Benedicta in for
elevenses."

"Oh, good! I'll call her. The poor child's
working away like a hero, all alone. I say,
Blessing! Coffee in five minutes. You are an
Angel-Blessing, really you are!"

"I've done a lot of work," and Benedicta showed
her trug, heaped with weeds. "I'll empty this and
then I'll come. I'd better wash before I eat."

"Not till Mr. Grandison has finished!"

"The kitchen sink will do for me. It's only clean
earth, but I don't want to eat it."

"This is mighty good of you, Miss Ellerton," Brian exclaimed, when he found Rachel presiding over a coffee-pot, and Damaris and Benedicta offering him biscuits, while the cats enjoyed saucers of milk in a corner.

"Ray really can make coffee," Damaris told him. "We've lived in France and Italy, and she didn't waste her time."

"It's most delicious coffee. I don't know why you should entertain me so bountifully."

"Since Lady Jen has bagged you for lunch we may surely give you your elevenses," Damaris said. "After this I'm going to help Benedicta with the weeding and you're going to see the Abbey from top to bottom. Top is the refectory, but bottom is underground. Wait till you see!"

"There's a wonderful Saxon crypt, and the old well round which the Abbey was built, and the tomb of the first Abbot," Rachel said.

Presently she led him off to see the wonders above and below ground, and the gardeners, much refreshed, returned to their weeding and clearing up.

CHAPTER V

A FRIEND FOR ROSEMARY

KENNETH MARCHWOOD's reaction to Jen's phone-call was completely satisfactory. "Capture him —keep him—chain him down! I'll talk for a week about Africa and we'll argue Kenya versus Rhodesia till I win. Any news of Brownie?"

"Not yet. She won't be home till two. I'm thinking about her all the time," Jen responded.

She turned to her guest when Kenneth had rung off, and repeated the message. "Ken is like me, thinking about our big little girl at school. He calls her Brownie, which was my nickname as May Queen; it fits her, for she's a little brown gipsy. It never suited me, but I wore a brown train, so I was known as Brownie. He really wants you to come, Mr. Grandison; he'll enjoy talking to you. I hope you'll stay for a few days. Will your people spare you?"

"They're used to doing without me," he smiled. "It fits rather well. Dad has to run over to Amsterdam to conduct his symphony at a concert, and Mother wants to go with him, so I was going to be on my own for the week-end."

"Ken will love to have you here. Is that the concert the Quellyns are off to to-morrow?"

"I believe they're all travelling together. Dad thinks a lot of Sir Ivor and they're friendly with Lady Quellyn, too."

"She lives next door; to us she is Joy. You came through her garden, and her twin girls are at school with our Rosemary."

"Brownie?" he questioned.

Jen laughed and agreed. "I must show you the rest of our Pieces of Eight. Katharine is four and a half, another little brown gipsy. Then there are twin boys, Chris and Barney, who are a year and a half old; and the infant is Barbara Rose. She's big and fair like me, and like all our five boys. Everybody shrieks at sight of her and scolds me for having an untidy family; I'm expected to have small dark girls. But she's rather a pet, and I'm quite fond of her, although she isn't the sixth boy I'd hoped for."

"I'm sure you are," Brian laughed.

It was plain to him during lunch that Jen's thoughts were elsewhere, and he challenged her on the subject at last.

"You're worrying about your little Brownie, aren't you, Lady Marchwood? But why? Why shouldn't she be happy at school?"

"I'm sorry. I apologise," Jen said contritely. "But she is rather heavily on my mind. I'm sure she'll be happy once she's used to school, but she's a queer little person, not exactly shy, but self-contained and reserved, and it may take her some time to settle down. She's a throw-back to my husband's family, in every way; not in the least

like Ken or me—we were never shy! She's had
so much illness that she has been with me, and
older people, a great deal, and she'll find it hard
to take her place among a crowd of girls."

"But with so many little brothers and
sisters——?" he began.

"Oh, she's all right with tinies! We've several
families of babies in the connection and Rosemary
is always good with them. You should see her
playing with Lady Kentisbury's four small
daughters—two sets of twins, with less than a
year between them! Or with our own tribe of
babies; Rosemary is a mother to them all. If
she could stay with Mike, who is three years
younger, she'd be happy; she'd forget herself in
taking care of him. But Mike will be with the
other small children; he doesn't need protecting.
He can take care of himself perfectly well. I'm
afraid Brownie would feel the wrench when he
had to go to the Kindergarten and she had to
stay with a crowd of strange girls. Oh, well!
I shall hear all about it in half an hour! Will you
go back to town, to make your plans?"

"My car is parked at the Abbey gate. And Miss
Damayris still has to show me round her garden,"
he explained. "What delightful girls those are
in the Abbey, Lady Marchwood! I'm fascinated
by them."

Jen gave him a quick look. "They're all well
worth knowing. Young Benedicta is a dear, and
Rachel is a most interesting girl. She has only
been here for fifteen months, but already she is

counsellor and friend to our younger folk; the schoolgirls take their troubles to her, and Benedicta has dubbed her our Abbot. We shan't keep Damaris long now; she'll be off to London for treatment and training. Rachel is going to miss her badly."

"I guessed as much. But her return will bring great joy to her friends in town. My Dad and Mother will be delighted to hear the news; I know how much they think of her."

"She'll have a great welcome," Jen agreed. "And she'll be very happy. Rachel will rejoice in her success, but she'll be lonely. Benedicta can't hope to take the place of Damaris. Let's go back to the Abbey! I'm going to stop the car and bring my two big children home through the park. The walk will be good for them; they're used to spending all day out of doors."

She was waiting by the Abbey wall long before the car could arrive. Rachel and Benedicta joined her, both eager to hear Rosemary's story, but Damaris carried Brian off to see the garden.

"Ray and Blessing will tell us about Rosemary. Come and see my baby sedums and heaths on Windermere and Wirral, and decide which you'll have in your rock-garden at Ambleside!"

Brian went eagerly. Rachel and Benedicta were delightful and interesting, but he had fallen under the spell of Mary Damayris and wanted nothing better than her company.

"Here they are! I'll stop the car," and Benedicta ran out into the road, waving her arms.

The man drew up and Jen called an explanation. "I'll take the children home by the garden, Henderson. You go on; they ought to have a walk."

"Mother, school's fun!" Michael shouted.

"I'm sure it is, laddie. Well, Brownie, did you like it?" Jen took her daughter's arm and drew her out.

"Oh, Mother, must we come home early?" Rosemary pleaded, springing down into the road. "None of the others do, and they were going to have cricket this afternoon. We didn't want to come home."

"That's good news!" Jen exclaimed, in great relief. "Then you thought it was fun, too, Brownie?"

"I didn't want to come away from Myonie."

"My—what?" Jen asked, slightly stunned.

Rachel, with dancing eyes, glanced at Benedicta, who grinned back at her, but they were careful not to interrupt.

"Brownie keeps on about Myonie," Mike grumbled.

"Her name's really Hermione," Rosemary explained at breathless speed. "But it's too long, and her mother calls her Hermy. I said she could be Hermy at home, but it wasn't grown-up enough for school, so we'd use the end part instead, and everybody began to call her Myonie; she liked it. She's Myonie Manley, and she's in my form. Her mother was a Queen, like you, Mother."

"Dear me! This is very intriguing!" Jen cried. "You haven't lost much time in making friends! Who is Hermione Manley? Which Queen was her mother?"

"She was shy." Rosemary went on with her story. "Mike had to go away, to be with the other little ones, and I felt a bit funny——"

"They're nice," Mike said. "We had great fun. And Miss Black's frightfully jolly."

"You felt a bit funny," Jen prompted her daughter. "What happened next? Did you see Myonie looking shy?"

"She was crying," Rosemary said simply. "She's only just eight and she hasn't anybody to play with at home, and she thought there were such lots of people. I felt like that, too, and then Rosalind came in—I mean Queen Lavender— and she told me Myonie's name and asked me to look after her. Lavender said: ' You aren't shy, Rosemary. You're used to taking care of people and Hermione is younger than you. Try to cheer her up and make her feel at home.' So I did. And—and that's all."

"You made friends," Jen supplemented. "And it cheered you up too, because you had to take care of Myonie. How clever and understanding of Queen Lavender! But tell me about Hermione. Who is her mother? I ought to know her, if she was a Queen. But I've never heard of Myonie before."

"They haven't been living here, but her mother

came sometimes for crownings; I've seen her. She was Queen Clover," Rosemary explained.

"Clover! The Queen after Maidie-Primrose!" Jen exclaimed. "A brown girl, who wore a dull pink train with four-leaved clovers on the border and big white clover flowers in the corners! She was younger than we were and we only saw her at coronations. So she has a daughter called Hermione! I never knew that before."

"She's Hermione Rose," Rosemary said. "I told her our baby was Barbara Rose, and that there were five younger than me. She said there couldn't be, but I told her their names, and she said she hadn't anybody. She had a little brother, but he died. Her daddy died, too; that's why they've come to live here, with her granny, so that Myonie can come to our school. She thinks I'm very lucky to have so many babies."

"You are very lucky," her mother assented. "Don't you ever forget it! Poor Clover! That's a sad story. Perhaps we can cheer her up. We wondered why she didn't come to Lavender's crowning. Hermione ought to have Aunty Rosamund for her god-mother, like Barbara and all our other Rose babies, but that can't be, or we should have heard about her long ago."

"I asked Myonie, and she said Aunty Ros— but she called her Lady Kentisbury—wasn't 'fishly her god-mother. Her mother thought a fearful lot of Queen Rose, when she was at school, and she'd have liked to be her maid-of-honour. But Aunty Ros didn't ask her; she didn't know how

much Myonie's mother admired her. So when
Myonie came she was called Rose after Aunty
Rosamund."

"She'll have to be an unofficial god-child! I'm
quite sure Aunty Ros will adopt her."

"Myonie would like that. Will you tell Aunty
Ros, Mother?"

"I'll ring her up to-night," Jen promised. "Was
Myonie—I like your name for her!—more cheerful
after you took charge of her?"

"Yes, a lot. But she didn't want me to come
home early. She's never played cricket and she
wanted me to show her how to bowl."

"Your cricket's all right, thanks to the coaching
your big brothers have given you! And you'd like
to stay at school all day?"

"Yes, please. Nobody else goes home early."

"We'll have to ask Father. But what about
Mike?"

"He could stay, too. The little ones have a
sleep after dinner; they have little beds—I saw
them. Then they have games till four o'clock.
Mike would like it."

"Would like it ever so much," Mike said sturdily.

"And can I have Myonie to tea?" Rosemary
begged.

"Oh, for sure! We must have Myonie *and* her
mother. Queen Clover must come, and we'll
collect the other Queens—Aunty Ros and Aunty
Maid and Aunty Joy and Aunty Joan. They'll
all bring little girls and we'll have a proper party
for Myonie."

"Oh, goody!" Rosemary gave a skip of excitement.

"This is a great weight off my mind!" Jen said solemnly, looking across at Rachel and Benedicta.

CHAPTER VI

A KEY FOR RACHEL

"MYONIE WANTS to see the Abbey. She's heard about it." Rosemary was chattering happily as Jen set out for home, calling a temporary farewell to Brian Grandison.

He rose from the rockery by which he had been kneeling. "Is this Brownie? Oh, yes, it most certainly is Brownie! And all's well?"

"All is very well. We've made a new friend and we're quite happy." Jen smiled in great relief.

Rosemary rushed off to seize Rachel's golden cat, who was dancing round his black foster-sister, while she crouched on the gravel drive with lashing tail.

"Golden Boy, shall I tell you about Myonie? She likes cats; hers is black, with white top-boots and a white shirt. I told her about my Ginger, but she'll like to see you too."

"Golden Boy has a new name." Rachel smiled down at the small girl. "Now that he's almost grown up it was time he had a real name; he can't go on being Boy for ever. So we call him Rory."

"Rory? That's a funny name!" Rosemary exclaimed.

"It's because he purrs in such a loud roar," Rachel explained seriously. "He's a regular roarer."

"So you call him Rory!" Rosemary chuckled. "I'll tell Myonie about Rory being a roarer!"

"Myonie and you seem to have endless points in common," Jen said. "Come and tell Ginger about her! Katharine wants to hear about school, too. Look at Mike! He's half-way home already!"

Mike, sturdily independent, had reached the Abbey gate and was clamouring to have it opened. Rachel let the little family party go through, and then came back to Benedicta.

"It will do Rosemary all the good in the world. Lady Jen is sure she's been dreading school. She'll be much better now that she's taken the plunge."

"Myonie has been a real blessing," Benedicta agreed.

The telephone rang in the Abbey and Rachel turned to the gate.

Damaris shot past her, in a wild, excited leap. "It may be for me."

"What is she expecting?" Benedicta asked.

"I've no idea. She hasn't said anything." Rachel looked troubled.

Damaris met them at the gate, her face radiant and full of excitement. "It was Madame. My letter caught the very early post and she's just had it. She wants to see me at once; she's terribly thrilled. She asked if I could go to-night."

"To-night!" It was a cry almost of tragedy from Rachel.

Brian and Benedicta looked at her quickly, and saw she was white, with startled eyes.

"Only just to have a talk!" Damaris said hurriedly. "I'd come back to-morrow. But she can't wait. She wants to see for herself. Oh, Ray, can't I go? I think I must go, Ray. *I* can't wait, either."

"I could run you up to town," Brian said. "And I could bring you back to-morrow, when I come to stay at the Manor. My mother would be delighted if you'd come to us for the night."

Damaris turned to him, her face ablaze with gratitude. "Would you? Take me to town and bring me back? Madame will give me a bed. Your car would be the most enormous help. You *are* good! Can you wait while I get into a frock and fling a few things into a bag? Thanks a million times! You don't mind, do you, Ray? You know I simply must go."

One second had been enough for Rachel. Her eyes were quiet again and her colour had come back. "Of course, you must go. Madame wants to talk things over with you. Run off and change! If Mr. Grandison will really take you to town, that will be a great help."

"I'll bring her back to-morrow," Brian said, as with a whoop of excitement Damaris was gone. "Miss Rachel, I hope you won't feel unhappy about her. Everybody will be very careful of her; she's rather a valuable person, isn't she?"

"Oh, I know she'll be all right! And she has

to go," Rachel said quietly. "Thank you for your help." She went after Damaris to the house, and they heard her call: "Can I do anything, Marry?"

Brian looked at Benedicta. "She doesn't want Mary Damayris to go, does she?"

"She wants her to go, but she's going to miss her terribly."

"Can't you fill the gap her sister will leave?"

"Oh, no! Nobody can do that. I'll be here, for company, and I'll take on the garden for Damaris, but I can't take her place. Rachel has promised to be happy about it," Benedicta said gravely. "She said it last night. But it's easier to say than to do. She knows it has to be and she won't spoil it for Damaris, but she's going to feel very bad."

Rachel came out again. She had herself well in hand by this time.

"Mr. Grandison, I want you to stay for tea, but Damaris won't hear of it. She's on fire with eagerness to reach Madame and show her what she can do and get her advice. Do you mind?"

"I sympathise in her eagerness," he laughed. "I can quite understand it. If tea seems imperative we'll stop somewhere on our way; I'd be proud to treat Mary Damayris to a drink! But it's more likely she won't want to spend time on it. I'll hand her over to Madame Roskova, and if she'll come to us for the night we shall be honoured. But I quite expect her friend and teacher won't give her up, even for bed. I'll do my best to return her safely to-morrow, Miss Rachel."

"You're more than kind! It really is a help to know you will take care of her."

Damaris came running out, a small case in her hand. "You can come to hear about the rest of the garden when you're staying at the Manor. Sir Ken can do without you for an hour, and Blessing can tell you things, if I'm not here. Do you mind if we go at once? I just can't wait to get to Madame!"

"We're going right now," he assured her. "We know you can't wait. Nothing matters but hearing what Madame has to say."

Damaris paused, on her way to the car. "Do you think I'm a little bit mad? If you knew—!"

"I think you're right," he assured her. "I'm all out to help, in any way I can."

"Oh, good! I'm not really a lunatic, but I've wanted it so much, and it is my whole life."

She went to the car, but turned at the Abbey gate. "Here, Ray, take this! I sha'n't ever want it again. It's yours now. Keep Blessing for the night, for company. She can have my bed." She tossed something to Rachel and ran to the car.

"What did you give your sister? And why will you never want it again?" Brian asked, as they set out.

"A key!" Damaris looked grim. "It's the key of the Abbot's oratory, and the oratory is where we go when things are too bad for words. The key was given to me so that I'd have a private place, a retreat, when I felt I couldn't bear things any longer; I've had some bad times, you know.

I used to shut myself in and weep on the floor. I'm afraid for Rachel; she feels things so terrifically. If she has to break her heart, she'll want to do it in the oratory."

"But she is willing you should go," he said quickly.

"Oh, yes! Things might be worse. Ray's awfully decent and she knows I have to go. If I were insisting on going against her will, that really would make a division between us, and that would break both our hearts. It's not as bad as that. She'll go with me in her mind; we won't really be separated. But all the same, Ray's going to want the oratory. I'm glad I remembered the key."

"You won't let the thought of her spoil your joy in this return to your old life?"

"Nothing could do that," Damaris said simply.

He gave her a quick glance. "It's a wonderful time for you."

"Oh, quite marvellous! Nice of you to understand! Now that we can't see Ray's tragic eyes, let's be jolly and enjoy it! I'm sorry about Ray, but she has the Abbey. It will comfort her quite soon."

CHAPTER VII

NIGHT IN THE ABBEY

RACHEL STOOD looking at the key. "Marry understands," she said to herself. "Well, that's something! I'd feel worse if it meant nothing to her."

"Is it——? Oh, I see! How thoughtful of Damson!" Benedicta exclaimed.

Rachel glanced at her. "You'll go on with your job, won't you? I know there's heaps to do. I'd better go in," and she disappeared through the Abbey gate.

Benedicta pursed her lips. "She can't go and cry in the oratory, for fear visitors come. It's hard on her. But I couldn't show tourists round. Ray's on duty; she'll have to wait. I can't help her. I'll carry on with that weeding."

Rachel stood looking at the telephone. "I'd better ring Lady Jen. It seems natural to tell her things, and she'll hear to-morrow, when Mr. Grandison comes back. She'd wonder why I hadn't said anything."

She rang up the Manor. "Lady Jen? Damaris has gone. I thought you'd better know."

"Gone? Oh, my dear, what do you mean?"

Rachel told what had happened and the plan

for the next day. There was a pause, while Jen took in the news. Then she said quietly, "That all seems very well arranged. One can sympathise in her excitement. What about you, Ray?"

"Nothing. I'm all right, Mrs. Brown."

"That old nickname always makes me laugh! Are you feeling very desolate?"

"Yes, Mrs. Brown."

"I was afraid you would. Could you come here for the night, when you close the Abbey to visitors?"

"Oh, no! It's a kind idea, but I must be here. Marry might ring up to tell me what Madame says. I don't really think it will occur to her, but if it does I wouldn't like her to get no answer."

"I see. Will you keep Benedicta for the night?"

"No." Rachel's tone was almost defiant. "Marry suggested it, but I don't want anybody. I'm perfectly safe; no one can get into the Abbey."

"I know, but I don't like to think of you all alone."

"I'd much rather, honestly. Don't worry about me. I wouldn't have told you, but I knew you'd hear it from Mr. Grandison to-morrow."

"Yes, of course. I say, Ray! I like him quite a lot."

"So do I. He seems kind and understanding."

"Wouldn't it be fun if Dammy-Marry married him and went to look after his rock-garden in the North? Or do you want him yourself?"

"Oh, no! I've married the Abbey. I won't have anyone else."

"I rather thought you felt like that. Well, Damaris, then."

"Oh, I wish she would!" It was a heartfelt cry from Rachel. "I'd feel so much happier about her! But I'm afraid she'll never marry. And I'm afraid of something else, Mrs. Brown."

"That he'll want her and break his heart if he can't get her?"

"Just that. He thinks she's marvellous."

"He's old enough to look after himself. You can't do anything. Perhaps he'll win her away from the stage."

"Dancing means so much to her. I haven't much hope." Rachel rang off and went to her work-room.

Benedicta, creeping to the gate to listen, heard the sound of the typewriter. "Oh, good! She's working. She said she was going to copy out a story. She won't have time to think."

By a great effort Rachel kept her mind fixed on the manuscript for an hour. Original work would have been impossible; she could not have lost herself in it. But, desperately determined to concentrate, she managed to type her story and even felt some satisfaction in the clean pages as she slipped them into a drawer and went to put on the kettle.

"Tea, Benedicta!" she called presently.

Benedicta came eagerly. "I'm always dying for it! Did you finish your story?"

"The typing's done. I still have to read it through. And I've done a letter to Marigold in

Ceylon, about the Coronation and telling her our news. Jansy will write, but Marigold will want to hear about Damaris from me. I rather hoped some tourists would come, but we're having a quiet day, so far as visitors are concerned. You heard what Marry said about the night?"

Benedicta glanced at her. "I heard. But you don't want me, do you?"

"I don't mean to be unkind, but I'd rather be alone. Do you mind?"

"No, but I'd like to be company for you. She didn't want you to be all on your own."

"It's perfectly safe. I don't want company. Don't tease me, Benedicta."

Benedicta said no more. She worked late, doing the weeding which Damaris had neglected; then she called good-night, but was not surprised to receive no answer. Rachel, released from duty, had taken off her white gown, pulled on a big coat and gone to the oratory.

Soberly, Benedicta went to her room in the village, and thought much before she slept of the girl who had gone from the Abbey and the girl who was left alone.

No schoolgirls came to the Abbey that night. Rachel was relieved and wondered if Jen had passed on the news to the Hall. Joy and Mary would be home by now; it was kind of them not to ring up and sympathise. She could guess how Jen would insist that she must be left in peace.

She sat on the floor in the Abbot's little room,

on the rug Damaris had placed there, and thought, heavily and desolately, of the changes that had come so suddenly. She was not the sort to cry easily, but a feeling of dead depression came down and seemed to crush her. There was nothing to cry about. It was right for Damaris to go back to her old life; it was necessary that she herself should stay in the Abbey. She wanted to stay; she wanted Damaris to go. But the separation hurt her; she could not take it lightly.

She rose at last, very cold and stiff, and went up the steps to the oratory, to kneel where the abbots had knelt and to pray, as they had prayed, for one who must leave the Abbey sanctuary and go out into the trials of the world.

Then, a little comforted, she went down to the garth, realising suddenly that she was shivering.

"I must have a fire and a hot drink," the thought. "It doesn't seem worth while cooking supper for myself, but I must do it. That's one of the things about which I'll have to be careful. I mustn't turn into an idiot who lives on tea and bread and butter. I'll have an egg, though it seems silly to do just one. I'd much rather creep into bed and eat a biscuit."

She paused on the garth, to let the silence and peace of the old place soak into her; the quiet was broken only by the hooting of an owl. At last she turned to her home within the walls.

Then she stopped, in great surprise and almost in fear, for light was streaming out into the passage, and the black kitten sat washing her face in the shining doorway, having obviously just been fed.

"Who? What? Marry?" she cried.

Mary Devine, Joy's secretary at the Hall, came to meet her.

"Forgive me, Ray! Jen told us your story, when we came home from The Pallant, and begged me to come and see that you were properly fed. She was afraid you'd go to bed without troubling about supper."

The rose-coloured curtains were drawn, a small fire flickered in the grate; the golden cat lay singing happily on the hearthrug, half asleep. With grave courtesy he came to meet Rachel, purring his usual noisy roar, and she bent and stroked his head and clapped his comfortable flanks.

The electric light was glowing under its crimson shade, and the table was laid for a meal for two, a bowl of three red rosebuds in the centre.

"Joy sent those," Mary explained. "They're early, aren't they? She cut all there were in the greenhouse for you."

"How kind!" Rachel stood and looked round. "Oh, Mary! It's home! When I think of the bustle and noise of London——!"

"But Damaris enjoys the rush and excitement," Mary reminded her. "You two are very different, you know. She'll be happy, and perfectly safe. Now, Ray, I was going to make an omelette as soon as you came in, but I know your omelettes are rather special. Would you prefer to do it yourself? Everything is ready."

Rachel flung off her coat. "I'll do it. Mary, you are good! Weren't you tired, after being out all day? And after last night?"

"Not a bit! I'm going to tell you about Maidlin and Baby Paul, when you've finished cooking."

"Yes, please. I want to hear all about our newest cousin."

"His father calls him Jackie-Paul. Maid is very happy and very proud of her boy. Shall I stay with you for the night? I brought a tooth-brush and a few things, in case you'd like to have me."

Rachel, busy with her eggs, smiled across at her. "There's no need, but I'd like you to stay. I thought I couldn't bear to have anybody, but you're rather a special person, like my omelettes, aren't you? It's a very dark night; I'd have to go with you through the garden, and then you'd have to come back with me, and we should never get to bed at all. Stay with me, Mary-Dorothy! You shall have one cat for company and I'll have the other. You'll tell me about Maid and the little girls and Jackie-Paul, and I'll tell you about Mr. Grandison's visit and more about Damaris."

CHAPTER VIII

MARY SPEAKS

"WERE YOU going to bed without any supper?"
Mary asked. "Jen was afraid you would."

"Too bad of Mrs. Brown! I was going to boil
an egg, though it seemed hardly worth while,
just for myself. Tell me about the twins and
Jansy at school! I was glad none of them came
to-night."

"They wanted to come," Mary said. "But
Rosalind—I mean Queen Lavender—persuaded
them to leave you in peace. She said—and we all
felt—that you wouldn't want them to-night.
School went off quite well. The twins are likely
to be picked for the junior cricket team and
they're highly delighted. Their cricket is really
good, especially Margaret's; the boys at the
Manor have coached them well."

"That sounds hopeful for the term."

"Everyone is complimenting Rosalind on the
way she dealt with Rosemary Marchwood, and
Jen is very grateful."

"By giving Rosemary somebody to look after,"
Rachel assented. "It was brilliant. Brownie
looked very well pleased with life."

"Yes, she has made a happy start. Jen hardly
dared to hope for it. Queen Lavender is being

thanked by everybody. Her first act as Queen, and a most successful one."

"Come and eat," Rachel said. "And then we'll sit over the fire, and nurse the cats, and talk. You've done a big thing for me to-night, Mary-Dorothy."

"By making sure you have a good supper?"

"More than that. When I came to the door and saw the light and the fire, and you, and Miss Nigger in the doorway, I knew how much it meant to me to have a home, even if it's a little one. Damaris doesn't care in the same way; she's been happy here, but she can be content to live anywhere, so long as she can have her dancing. Hotels or rooms satisfy her; she isn't critical."

"But you want your home," Mary agreed. "Biddy and I were like that. She was ambitious and she wanted to get on in her job; she didn't mind transplanting herself to France, or anywhere, if it meant promotion. I felt lost, when I was uprooted from our flat in town; and then I was—oh, so happy!—when I saw the beautiful rooms Joy and Jen had planned for me at the Hall. I settled down and felt I had a real home, as you have done here. Quite like you and Damaris!"

"But Biddy has her own home now, and her husband and children, in France. If only Marry would settle down, too! I'd be so much happier about her——"

The telephone rang. Rachel, looking startled, picked up the receiver and listened intently.

"How nice of you, Marry! Yes—yes—I see. Yes, that's good. Thanks so much for telling me. Oh, I'm all right! No, not Blessing; I sent her home. But Mary-Dorothy came, to stand over me till I had had a good supper, and she's going to stay. Yes, much better than Benedicta, though I love her, too. But I'd rather have Mary. Quite a good supper, thank you. An omelette; I made it. Yes, the cats and the Abbey are all right. Till to-morrow, then; and good luck to you in the morning!"

She put down the receiver and came back to the table. "Could you follow that, Mary-Dorothy?"

"Most of it," Mary smiled. "What is her news?"

"I'm glad Marry rang; I really didn't expect her to think of it. Madame and Antoine are in the seventh heaven of delight, at the thought of having her back. They're going to revive *The Goose-girl* for her; it hasn't been shown since Daphne Dale married. And the fairy ballet, *Rainbow Corner*. Later on, when Marry is used to dancing again, they want her to take the leading role in a new ballet. But all that's in the future. To-morrow Madame is going with her to see Sir Robert Duncan, who attended Marry when the accident happened; she calls him Sir Bob. They've rung up and made an appointment. He'll advise her about the immediate present; Madame thinks massage and special baths may be helpful. They want to have her as well and fit as possible. After a course of treatment she'll begin working in earnest, under Madame's special care; they won't let her dance until they are sure she can stand the strain of it."

"She'll be well looked after. You've no need to worry about her."

"I know. But it's strange without her. I don't like it."

"Could you come and live at the Hall? No one would run away with the Abbey in the night. Our schoolgirls and babies would keep anybody cheerful."

"And leave my home?" Rachel asked reproachfully. "No, Mary-Dorothy! I'd rather be here. This is my place and my job."

"You must remember," Mary said presently, as they sat over the fire, each nursing a happy singing young cat, "that you have your work and it can be done at home. You can write better in the Abbey than in hotels. It keeps you content here. Damaris has a very great gift and she must use it; it would be a sin to stifle or neglect it. She can only use it in London, or touring about the country. The gift is so great and so compelling that she'll give up everything for it. One part of her may be craving for a settled home, but it has to be denied for the sake of the gift."

Rachel stroked a soft little black head and gazed into the fire. "Then she wouldn't be right to give up her dancing to have a home of her own?"

"I don't pretend to be very wise," Mary began, "but——"

"Oh, but you are!" Rachel assured her earnestly. "Tell me what you think!"

"I should say she would be wrong to deny her gift its full expression just for the sake of ease and comfort; to settle down at home and enjoy herself. She couldn't do it. But if she loved some man, I'd say she was right to give up even her dancing for him. I'd think it was wrong to let her career spoil the happiness of two lives."

"Madame Roskova feels like that. She left the stage for years and lived a private life. She said she was glad Daphne Dale should give up her career for marriage, and she wished Damaris could do it too."

"Because it's a more all-round complete life," Mary assented. "You can't deny that Damaris is one-sided. At present only her artist part is being developed. We shall see where she ends. You regret her return to London, Ray; but suppose there is someone she will meet there, who can give her that full and complete life? She might never meet him here. If you could keep her in the Abbey you might shut her out from her real future. You must let her go, and be happy about it so that she can be happy, too; and then you must wait and trust. There may be big things before her; she must go out and seek adventure. You know how love and marriage have developed Maidlin, who was far too much the artist at one time. She's still an artist and a much finer one than she would have been if she hadn't met Jock. She'll be singing again in public in the autumn, when Jackie-Paul can be left for a few hours; and everyone says how much her voice has deepened since she married."

"Marry couldn't go on dancing, if she married," Rachel observed. "I believe some people do, but it doesn't seem reasonable to me."

"Unless she married a dancer. We can't plan that. Ray, dear, she is using the gift God gave her, in the new power which has been given back to her. Surely you can trust her to Him, for her future?"

Rachel gazed down at sleeping Miss Nigger. "Yes," she said at last. "I see that, Mary-Dorothy. Yes, I will give her up and believe all will be for the best. I meant to do it, and to try to be happy about it, for her sake, but it was going to be an effort. You've made me see it in a new light. Thank you, Mary! I shall be happier now."

"I'm very glad. I do hope you will," Mary said earnestly. "Our joy over this wonderful news has been clouded by the thought of you. Joy and Jen and I, and Maidlin, when Jen rang up and told us, have all felt the same. 'But what about Rachel?' Maid said at once; and we agreed. If you can let her go happily, it will ease all our minds."

"How kind of you to care!" Rachel exclaimed, much touched. "And to know how I should feel!"

Presently she looked up again. "I'm afraid Mr. Brian Grandison would like to be the man to tempt Marry away from her stage career."

"Don't you like him? Jen seemed to think well of him."

"I like him very much. I'd marry Damaris to him, if I could. But she isn't thinking of marriage, and I'm afraid he may get hurt."

"Give her time," Mary advised. "She hardly knows him yet. He may awaken new thoughts in her."

"He thinks he knows her," Rachel remarked. "He's very taken with her. But we must leave it to him. It will take a lot to drag Marry from the stage! I'll wash up and leave the house tidy, and then we'll stroll in the cloisters and feel the peace of the Abbey. Come and see how Rory helps me!"

"You'll let me help, too, I hope," Mary said. The golden cat followed them to the tiny kitchen and jumped up on the table.

"Watch him!" Rachel said. She washed their dishes and cups and then took the tea-cloth which Mary was using. "Let me do the rest."

Golden Rory had been perched on the edge of the table, as close to her as he could go. Now, as she seemed to ignore him, he put out a soft little paw and pulled the towel out of her hand. It fell on the table, and he planted his foot firmly on it and gazed adoringly up at his mistress, in smiling triumph.

Rachel laughed. "I wasn't talking to you, was I, dearest? He always drags the cloth out of my hands, Mary. He insists on being one of the family; he won't be left out." She fondled the soft golden head and stroked the smooth back and looked down into the deep yellow eyes.

"He really loves you," Mary said.

"I think he does. He's going to be quite a companion, when Damaris goes."

"More than the black girl?"

"Much more," Rachel said firmly. "Miss Nigger has other friends, especially at the farm. She puts up with me; I'm useful to provide meals and beds! But Golden Rory likes to be with me, and he insists on being noticed. There, dear! Will that do? Now come out into the Abbey with Mary-Dorothy and me, and then we'll all go to bed!"

CHAPTER IX

BRIAN SUGGESTS A HOLIDAY

"I'M DISAPPOINTED in Sir Bob!" Damaris announced, jumping from the car at the Abbey gate.

"Sir Bob is very wise," Brian Grandison said, with enthusiasm, following her.

Rachel had been waiting for them. "Have you been arguing all the way from town? Thank you a thousand times, Mr. Grandison! Now, what's this about Sir Bob? Won't he let you dance, Marry?"

"Not yet; he was quite fierce about it. I'm to have three months' special treatment at a place in Oxford; he's writing to them. He says they can do just as much for me as anyone in town, and I'm to live at home with you and be out in the garden, and get as well and fit as possible. After all that, I'm to go away for a month, for a holiday, before I begin work with Madame; he absolutely insists on it. Even then, he'll only let me start in earnest if he's satisfied; if I cut out the holiday or shirk the treatment he'll have no more to do with me."

"Madame won't risk that," Rachel said. "I'm very grateful to Sir Bob. You'd rush into full-time work at once, if you were allowed, and then you'd overdo things and put yourself back for months."

"It's horrible of him," Damaris grumbled. "I don't want to mess about all summer! I've had a holiday for a year and a half."

Rachel looked at Brian. "May we give you that cup of tea, that you couldn't wait for yesterday? You could spare half an hour before going to the Manor."

"Thank you very much," he said. "I'll enjoy it, Miss Rachel."

"Where's Blessing?" Damaris demanded. "Don't say she's deserted my garden the moment my back was turned!"

"She's gone to Kentisbury. The Countess rang up and invited her for the day and sent the car for her. Benedicta loves going to the Castle to see all the babies, and she said—if you could have a day in town, she could have one in Sussex. She'll be home about six."

"Slacker! She ought to stick to the job."

"Will you wander round the garden, while I make the tea? The kettle must be nearly boiling." Rachel turned to Brian.

"No tourists?" he smiled.

"Not at present. I may have to leave you at any moment, but Damaris will look after you. I had two parties this morning; quite pleasant folk and very understanding."

"You must have had great experience of all sorts of people. Mayn't I help to get the tea?"

"You may come in," Damaris said. "Your help

won't be worth much; you'd better leave it to us. Oh, Ray knows all about people! This is the ideal job for a novelist. She has a constant stream of new types and characters passing before her eyes."

"Some are very appreciative and enjoy it. Others don't show much feeling for the Abbey; but they're all interesting," Rachel said, leading the way. "I soon learnt when to take trouble and when it would be just waste of time."

"It keeps you tied to the job," he said. "Don't you ever want to escape?"

"The Abbey is only open from ten till six. In summer I have plenty of time for walks or for the garden. In winter we close at dusk; we can't show people round in the dark, in spite of the lights at certain places."

"But what about holidays? Don't you ever go away?" he asked, looking with real pleasure at the cosy room and the table laid for tea.

"Lovely roses!" Damaris exclaimed. "Where did you steal them?"

"Mary brought them last night. Lady Joy sent every one she had in her greenhouse. They've opened a lot to-day."

"Were they to comfort you because I'd skipped off and left you, or to congratulate me on my good news?"

"Mary didn't say. Both, I expect." Rachel removed a mingled mass of black and golden cat from the couch. "Out you go! You shouldn't be in here when the sun's shining. Have a game on the garth and get yourselves nicely aired. Sit down, Mr. Grandison. Everything's ready except the teapot."

"I'll make the tea." Damaris threw off her coat. "Mr. Grandison wants to talk to you. I've heard his opinions in the car."

"What do you do about holidays, Miss Rachel?" Brian asked again. "Can't anyone take your place?"

"There's a woman in the village who has acted as guide, but she won't take on the job for long at a time. But we haven't wanted holidays," Rachel said. "We've been so glad just to be here. We did think of going home, last autumn; I mean to Cumberland. That will always be ' home ' to us. But the plan fell through. Perhaps now——" and she looked thoughtfully at Damaris.

"She must have a holiday," he said eagerly. "Couldn't you get that woman to take over the Abbey, and both of you go north? I'd go at the same time, and you could help me to plan my rock-garden."

Rachel's eyes gleamed, as she stood putting milk in the cups. "That's rather a good idea," she said sedately. "No other place would do Marry so much good as Grasmere."

"Her native air, where she was born," he agreed warmly.

The girls laughed and looked at one another. "Don't you think it!" Damaris mocked. "We were born in New York. I began dancing there, when I was eight. We came home to the aunts at the farm when I was nine and Ray was ten;

and they put a stop to my dancing, and I only began again when I was sixteen."

"Thanks to a dear little Frenchman in Annecy," Rachel added.

"The world owes a lot to the little Frenchman," Brian said. "All the same, Cumberland is home to you, and it is where Mary Damayris must go for her holiday. Will you think over my plan, Miss Rachel?"

"I'd have to consult Mrs. Raymond; the owner of the Abbey, you know. I'd like to smell the fells again!" There was a wistful note in Rachel's voice.

"I'm sure you both ought to go to see your hills," Brian urged.

"Fells!" The girls spoke together.

He raised his brows. "You must instruct me in these matters."

"You'll understand, when you've seen them," Damaris told him. "Ray, will you wear your shorts for climbing?"

"I'll leave the shorts to you. Mine wouldn't fit now, and I'm not going to get new ones for a week or two."

"Sir Bob said a month or six weeks," Damaris said indignantly. "I'll need six months' hard work with Madame. It will be after Christmas before there's any *Goose-girl*. Rotten!"

"I want to see you as *The Goose-girl*," Brian admitted. "It seems a long while to wait."

"It's much worse for me," she retorted. "I shan't feel so bad once I start with Madame.

I shall go to see the ballet at night and I'll be right in the middle of things again. But I do feel mad at having to waste three months here, on baths and massage, and then another whole month doing nothing!"

Brian glanced at Rachel, and saw her lips pinch.

"You're a hard-hearted young woman," he said. "Can't you see your sister's point of view? She's rejoicing that she's going to have you for one more summer."

"Oh, bother!" Damaris groaned.

"It's all right," Rachel said quickly. "I want you to go back, Marry, and nobody's going to be as proud of your success as I shall be. But as I've had to accept the thought of losing you, you may as well put up with the thought of having one more summer with me."

Damaris gave her a sudden grin. "O.K., old dear! I'll do it. I won't grouse any more. Sir Bob has spoken and I must make the best of it. Mr. Grandison, you'd better be a good boy and run off and amuse Sir Kenneth Marchwood. He'll think you're lost."

"That's rude, Marry. I apologise for her, Mr. Grandison."

" I expect he likes it," Damaris said lightly. "I'm going to get into working kit and do the weeding that wretched Benedicta is neglecting."

"I shall come along to-morrow, to hear more about rock-plants," said Brian.

"Although I'm so rude?"

"You were right. I like it," he told her.

"You don't know what I could do, if I tried."

"I can stand it. Thank you for a delightful tea, Miss Rachel."

Rachel went with him across the garth and down the tresaunt. "Can you find your way? You must forgive Damaris. She's over-excited."

"It's no wonder! It's a great time for her. Yes, I remember all this; I shall find my way without any difficulty. Some day I must thank Lady Quellyn for allowing me to cross her lawn so often."

"It's the recognised path from the Manor to the Abbey. The road goes a long way round. Tell Lady Jen about Damaris and Sir Bob, and give her our love." And Rachel closed the garden gate behind him.

CHAPTER X

RODDY'S PLACE IN THE FAMILY

BENEDICTA, at the Castle, was present at a curious incident, which interested her greatly.

She had first known Kentisbury in the early days of the Countess's marriage, when the heir to the title had been little Roderick Kane, a two-year-old second cousin of the Earl. Roddy was also Countess Rosamund's half-brother, and she was his guardian, as his mother lived in India. Roddy, learning to talk, had called his big sister Yoz or Yozzie; then her own children had come, and he had been taught to call her Mother.

"It would be altogether too difficult to have Roddy saying 'Rosamund,'" Lady Kentisbury had explained. "We should have Hugh copying him in no time; it wouldn't do. I'll tell Roddy all about it when he is old enough to understand. I've been far more of a mother to him than his real one."

Tall, fair, and handsome, dressed in blue, Rosamund met Benedicta in the quadrangle of the Castle and took her to the Children's Garden, enclosed by a high box hedge, to see Roddy and Hugh playing with boats. Big Twins, who were called Rosabel and Rosalin, and were almost

three years old, were building a house for their
teddy-bears in the sandpit, and the tinies, Rosanna
and Rosilda, who were just two, were crawling
after a big coloured ball on the lawn.

"I like the blue rompers," Benedicta laughed.
"How much alike they all are, with their yellow
heads!"

"And blue eyes. The tinies call themselves
Zanna and Zilda," the Countess said. "You shall
play with them later on. Come into the rose-
garden; we have two or three early roses coming
out. We'll have our elevenses there."

They were sitting with coffee cups and cakes
under an arch which would soon be covered with
yellow roses, when Roddy burst stormily into the
garden, unheeding Nurse's warning that "My
lady has a visitor."

"Don't care. I want her," Roddy flung over his
shoulder. "Mother——"

"It's all right, Nanny," Rosamund said. "Let
him stay. I thought he had something on his
mind."

She held out her hand to Roddy, who, checked
in his wild rush, was breathless and panting.

"Shall I go?" Benedicta asked hurriedly.

"No, my dear. Roddy won't mind. Sit quiet
and don't interrupt. It may be useful to have
you here. We must have this out. I've been
expecting it."

"Mother, who am I?" Roddy demanded.

"Who are you, laddie? You're Roderick Geoffrey
Kane, and a very fine name it is."

"Is it my real name?"

"Of course it is. Your father chose it for you.
He said: 'If we have a little boy, he must be
called Geoffrey Kane, because that's the name of
all the boys in our family. But he can have
another name as well, so that he won't get mixed
with all the other Geoffreys.' Hugh is called
Geoffrey-Hugh, you know."

"Do you mean Daddy?" Roddy's eyes searched
her face anxiously.

The answer came in a completely matter-of-fact
tone. "No, not Daddy. You had another father
once, but he died before you were born."

"Then he wasn't much use to me!"

"Oh, yes, he was. He gave you your fine name.
You might not have been called Geoffrey Kane;
you must be proud of it."

"Then Daddy isn't—isn't——"

"Not your only father," Rosamund said quietly.
"But nobody could have been a better Daddy for
you."

Roddy was staring at her fixedly. "Then is
that why——?"

"Tell me, Roddy. What put all this into your
head?"

"Those people yesterday. They looked at Hugh
and they said: 'This is Lord Verriton,' and then
they looked at me and they said: 'And this is
Roddy Kane.' Isn't it more important to be
Lord Verriton?"

"In one way, yes, it is," Rosamund assented,

keenly interested to see how he had grappled with the problem.

"Well, I'm lots bigger than Hugh. Why aren't I the lord? And they called the girls 'Lady Rosalin' and 'Lady Rosabel.' Why can't I be something too?"

"You're something all right, but it's a long story." Rosamund's arm drew him close to her. "We've been waiting till you were ready to hear it. You must have heard Hugh called Verriton often, Roddy, but you didn't take any notice. It's the name given to the first boy in the Earl of Kentisbury's family, and all his little girls have to be called 'Lady.'"

"Then I'm not—not one of the family?" Suddenly Roddy's brave voice broke. "I've been thinking it must be that." He struggled gamely for self-control. "I forgot, when those people went away, and then I remembered again."

"You are one of the family; very much so! But you aren't Daddy's eldest son. Shall I tell you the story?"

Roddy hid his face against her. "Yes, please. I —I wish I belonged, like the rest do."

"I'll tell you who you really are. You're Daddy's little cousin, Roddy."

Roddy's head came up with an astonished jerk. "But how? Then—then I do belong to the family?"

"Oh, yes! Did you think we had just picked you up in the street somewhere? Dear boy, you have only to look at yourself in a glass! I don't suppose you ever do, but you're exactly like Hugh and the little girls, and like me, and like Daddy. You're a real Kane; anyone would know you were one of the family."

"Would they? I never thought of that."

"You go and stand beside Hugh, in front of a big mirror, and you'll see what I mean."

"I'm glad I belong," Roddy said. "But I wish Daddy was my real father."

"No one could have been a nicer father for you," Rosamund said cheerfully. "Your own father died, and then you were born, and your mother wanted to go——"

"Then you aren't—oh, you are my mother!" Roddy cried, and hid his face again.

"I've been your mother ever since you were a few weeks old. Your first mother went to live in India and she couldn't take a tiny baby there. You were a delicate baby; you needed English air and English sun and English milk; you'd have died quite soon in India."

He was tense with interest; she could feel it in his body. She went on quietly.

"So your mother gave you to me, when you were very, very small, and said I could be your mother. Then I decided to marry Daddy and come to live here; and what do you think Daddy said? He said: ' Here are we, you and I, with this great big castle and no children in it. And there's my little cousin, Roderick Geoffrey Kane, with no house and no daddy. Why shouldn't he come and live with us? It would make the castle much

more homelike to have a boy living in it.' Don't
you think that was rather nice?"

"Yes," Roddy whispered. "But when you had
Hugh and the others, did you still go on wanting
me? You've heaps of children now."

"Listen, Roddy!" Rosamund spoke very
earnestly. "Before we came here, you and I
lived together in a tiny little house, just a cottage,
and I did everything for you—washed you and
dressed you and fed you, made and washed and
ironed your baby clothes, put you out in the
garden in the morning and took you up to my
room at night. You slept beside my bed, and if
you cried I could put out my hand and touch you.
I used to feel for you in the dark, to make sure
you were really there, because it was so wonderful
to have a boy of my own, and I sang you to
sleep——"

"Did you want to have me?" Roddy cried.
"Wasn't it just that you felt you had to?"

"I wanted you more than anything in the world.
I had a special little song for you, and the chorus
was, 'Baby Alone and I.' It used to put you to
sleep."

"Sing it to me!"

"Some day, perhaps," Rosamund laughed. "I've
almost forgotten it. I never sang it for any of the
others, for it didn't fit. There was no 'Baby
Alone and I,' when Hugh came! It was your own
song."

"I'm glad about that. But—but all that, what
you said—washing me and doing my clothes and

my food—that's Nanny's work," Roddy protested.

Rosamund smiled. "It's Mother's work. But you have grown up in a family where the mother has outside things to do; people to help and to look after. You know how much I have to be out with Daddy? I couldn't do all that baby work as well, and so we have Nanny, and Agatha and Hyacinth to help. That's what I want you to see, Roddy. These children have had to be brought up by nurses, so that I could help Daddy in the outside things that have to be done. But there was no Nanny when you were little, so I did everything for you, far more than I've been able to do for these other children. That's a fact that nothing can ever alter. With you I had the real fun of having a baby all to myself. In some ways you'll always be more my own boy than any of the rest, because of those months when we lived in the tiny house together."

"Then I am your boy?" Roddy whispered.

"Very much so. You're our adopted boy; that means that when we didn't expect to have a boy of our own we chose you to belong to us."

Roddy looked up suddenly. "She can't come and take me away? That other mother, I mean? She didn't die, did she?"

"Oh, no! She lives in India. But she can't take you away. You belong to me; the papers making you mine are locked up in the lawyer's office. Nobody can take you away until you want to go."

"I'll never want to go!"

"Oh, yes, you will! Quite soon, too. You're going to school, to prepare for college, and then you'll go to Dartmouth to learn to be a sailor. And then you'll go on a ship and sail round the world and have adventures. Hugh can't do that. He must stay at home and learn to look after Kentisbury, as Daddy does. No going to sea for Lord Verriton!"

Roddy looked thoughtful. "I'd rather be me and go to sea."

"Of course you would. You'll have much more fun, in lots of ways. But there's one thing you haven't asked, Roddy. Why do you think your mother gave you to me? Why did she choose me to look after you?"

"I supposed you were there and you said you'd like to have me."

"That was true, but there was a bigger reason. It will seem funny to you at first, but I'll tell you how it happened. Roddy, boy, I'm your big sister!"

"My *sister*?" Roddy's cry of amazement rang out. "Oh, but you can't be! You're too old for a sister!"

"I'm not as old as you think! But it doesn't happen very often that a boy has the luck to have a big sister twenty years older than himself. Your first father was my father too, Roddy."

"Gosh, how odd!" Roddy stared at her incredulously. "And that other mother, too?"

"Oh, no! My mother died and my father found somebody else and married her, and she was your mother. I'm your half-sister, really; that's what we call it, when we had the same father, but different mothers. But never mind about that! You're my brother all right. All my life, Roddy, I wanted a baby brother or sister. The girls at school used to talk about their babies at home, and I was always a little lonely because I hadn't anybody. When I was quite big and had done with school, my mother died, and I was still more lonely. I had plenty of lovely kind friends, but there was nobody really belonging to me except my father, and he was far away in India; I didn't know him very well. Then he got married again and then he died; and then—think how marvellous for me, Roddy!—I heard there was a baby boy—my little brother come at last!"

"And it was me!" Roddy shouted, in wild excitement. "*I* was your little brother, come at last!"

Rosamund caught him to her and hugged him. "You were! I never was so happy about anything before. So when your mother went back to India, of course she gave you to me. Who should bring up a boy but his big sister?"

"Oh, yes!" Roddy accepted this at once. "You aren't Hugh's big sister, as well as his mother, are you?"

"Of course not. I'm nobody's sister but yours."

"Nobody's at all?"

"Nobody's, Roddy. I never had a brother or sister till you came."

"Then you do belong to me!" Roddy exulted

in the thought. "If you're Mother, then I have to go shares in you with Hugh and Big Twins and the tinies. I only have a little bit of you! But when you're a sister, do you belong to nobody but me?"

"As a sister, I belong to nobody but you, and no one else has any share in me," Rosamund said, much amused.

"Goody! I'm glad you're my sister. Shall I call you that?"

"We'd rather you didn't, for a little while longer. Some day, when you've been away to school and come back for holidays and everybody's rather more grown-up, you'll call me Rosamund, as Daddy does. But——"

"Rosamund! It does sound odd!" Roddy eyed her in amusement.

"You used to try to say it, but it was too hard and all you could manage was Yoz or Yozzie."

"How awful! That's ugly," Roddy laughed.

"So we changed to Mother. And we would like you to go on calling us Daddy and Mother, at present. You must know by now that Hugh copies you in everything, Roddy."

Roddy grinned. "He tries to do what I do. It wouldn't be proper for him to say Rosamund, would it?"

"It wouldn't do at all. And we don't want to tell him about it till he's older. He's only four; he couldn't understand."

Roddy looked mysterious. "No, all those little children couldn't understand. We'll keep it a secret. I'll call you Mother, but you'll know I really mean Big Sister."

"Don't forget! Rosabel is very quick; she'd want to know what you meant."

"It must be a secret," Roddy said decidedly. "A secret for you and me and Daddy. We won't tell those other little children yet."

Rosamund stifled a laugh. "That's a clever lad! There's one thing I haven't told you, Roddy."

"Something as nice as being your little brother?"

"As you are my brother, you can't be Hugh's or Rosabel's brother. You see that, don't you?"

"I always thought I was." Roddy grinned again. "Aren't I anything to them?"

"You're their uncle, my boy."

"Their *uncle*?" Roddy's eyes widened. "Like Daddy is Cousin Rosalind's uncle? Oh, but I can't be! I'm not old enough."

"Being old has nothing to do with it. My brother, old or young, is uncle to my real children."

"Golly, what sport!" Roddy murmured, fascinated by the idea. "Am I all their uncles?"

"Uncle to all the children, you mean? Of course you are."

"Uncle to all those little children!" Roddy's tone was full of amazement.

"Hugh is your nephew. The small girls are your nieces. But don't bother about it just now. I want you to know what a big place you have in the family, that's all."

"Your only little brother," Roddy mused, much impressed by his own importance. "And your first boy, in that little house when it was just us two together. And the boy Daddy wanted in his house, and his little cousin. And uncle to all those little children! I am one of the family, aren't I?"

"You are," Rosamund assured him laughing. "Here's Daddy coming to look for us. Ask him if you are one of the family!"

CHAPTER XI

"MY LADY'S LITTLE BROTHER"

ROSAMUND LAY BACK in her chair and smiled at Benedicta. "I'm tired! But I think I said the right things. I've been afraid I should make a mess of it when the time came."

"You did it beautifully," Benedicta exclaimed. "I was afraid he'd have an awful shock."

"Only a little one, I think. He was distressed for a moment, but he'll be happy about it now. I'm thankful it's over. Listen to his excitement!"

"Daddy! You did want me in your house, didn't you?" And Roddy poured out a jumbled tale of being an only little brother, a wanted boy, and an uncle to a crowd of little children.

Rather stunned to hear his large family of small people referred to thus, Lord Kentisbury sat on a garden seat and put his arm round the boy. "So the great secret is out at last?" He smiled across at his wife. "And are you going to be a good uncle for Hugh and the little girls, Roderick?"

"I'll try. You did want me, didn't you?" Roddy asked earnestly. "Thank you for having me in your house, Daddy."

"Such a big empty house, until we brought you

here! Are you going to help us, Roddy? You've
been quite a help already."

"Me? How can I? Oh, do you mean by taking
care of all the little children? Mother calls
them my somethings-or-other."

"Your nephews and nieces. Don't you see how
much you matter to the family? Think what it
would be like for Hugh, if you weren't here!"

Roddy thought over the idea. "You mean, if
there were only Hugh and Big Twins and the
tinies? It would be jolly dull for him, wouldn't
it? Nobody to play with."

"Only nurses and small girls. Hugh needs a
boy; he's been lucky to have you. You make it a
much nicer family, just by being here."

"Two boys, and then two lots of girls," Roddy
assented. "One boy would be dreadfully dull. Yes,
I see. It's a good thing I'm here."

"It may not always be a good thing," his adopted
father warned him. "Hugh looks up to you and
tries to be like you in everything. What about it,
Roddy? Are you going to be a good uncle for
him?"

Roddy shot a look at him. "You mean, make
him be sensible and not let him do silly things?"

"Or bad things. That's what I mean."

"Nanny calls it ' setting a good example to the
younger ones.' She often says it," Roddy informed
them. "I didn't listen very much before, but I
will now. I won't let Hugh learn bad things from
me, Daddy."

"Good! Then you'll be a real help to us. And

we'll go on as Mother and Daddy, till the rest of the family are old enough to understand, won't we?"

"It's to be a secret from all the little children." Roddy's tone was full of importance. "Does Nanny know?"

"Oh, yes! It's only a secret from those who are too small to understand," said the Earl. "If you ask any of our people who you are, they'll say: ' You're my lady's little brother.' That's their name for you."

"My lady's little brother! It's a nice name," Roddy said, with dignified approval.

"Things will be all right now." Rosamund turned to Benedicta again. "It's a load off my mind. I've been dreading the explanations, for fear I couldn't make him happy about it. I didn't want Roddy to suffer. Now you can help me by telling the story at the Abbey. I shall ring them up and say all is well, but Joy and Jen and Mary will want to know more about it. Give them any details you can; they'll sympathise. I'm seeing Maidlin to-morrow, so she'll hear the whole story. Joan will want to know, too; I'll see her on my way to Maid's place. Will you be my messenger to those at the Abbey?"

"I'll love to tell them all I can," Benedicta said fervently. "I hope the thought of being an uncle won't weigh on Roddy too heavily!"

Rosamund smiled. "It won't age him very much, but it may restrain him from too violent mischief. Hugh admires him so intensely that it is really important Roddy should be a good uncle. Now tell Geoffrey and me all the news! We want to hear about Mary Damayris. And Rachel; what will she do? Surely she won't leave the Abbey?"

"Damaris says she won't have her and she must stay. We talked about it, and Rachel promised to be happy, but she didn't look awfully happy yesterday, and it was a shock when Damaris went off to town with Mr. Grandison."

"What is he like? Jen spoke of him, when she rang up to tell me of Rosemary's new friend at school. I'd heard of the child; at a crowning some years ago Clover said to me: 'I've a daughter, and I've called her after you.' I said: 'Nice of you!' and sent the babe a present, a woolly suit; but then Roddy came and in all that excitement I forgot Clover's little Rose-girl. Eight years old, Jen said; I know Clover married early. I must see her and Hermione Rose. Look at those two, talking together! Wouldn't you think they were father and son?"

Lord Kentisbury and · Roddy were deep in earnest conversation. "Some day," Roddy's clear little voice came across the garden, "I'm going to be Admiral Sir Roderick Kane. Mother and I have been talking about it."

"That will mean hard work and being a very fine sailor," the Earl said seriously. "But I don't see why you shouldn't manage it one day. Now I want to talk to Benedicta, so suppose you go back to the sand-pit."

"May I tell Nanny about being my lady's little brother?"

"Nanny knows. But you may tell her that you know all about it now."

"But don't say it before Hugh and Rosabel, Roddy," Rosamund reminded him.

Roddy waved his hand in a reassuring gesture. "Those little children are too young to understand."

Rosamund and Benedicta followed him to the arch under the box-hedge, which led to the Children's Garden, and heard the loud whisper with which he greeted Nanny. Knowing very well what had been happening, she was looking anxious, but one glance at his excited face satisfied her.

"Nanny! Oh, Nanny, isn't it fun? Mother's my big sister! But don't tell all the little children. They're too young; they wouldn't understand."

Agatha, the second nurse, heard and collapsed into giggles.

Roddy looked at her coldly. "Don't tell them," he insisted.

"We won't say anything, Roddy. But you can talk about it to us when the babies aren't here," Nanny said. "It's too wonderful to be kept to yourself, isn't it?"

"It isn't funny." Roddy stared at Agatha wrathfully. "It's fun! But it isn't funny."

"Not funny at all. It's very nice. Agatha only laughed because you sounded suddenly so grown-up."

"Oh, was that it? I am grown-up. I'm all their uncles," Roddy said haughtily.

"Of course you are." Nanny looked sternly at Agatha, who showed signs of another collapse. "You'll be a very good uncle, I'm sure. And when Hugh is as old as you are now, we'll tell him all about it."

"Will he call me Uncle Roderick?"

"I can't say. But you'd better not insist on it," Nanny warned him. "Uncles are supposed to tip their nephews; give them presents of money, you know. Your nieces might expect it too, and it would be expensive."

"There's too many of them. I couldn't give them all presents! I might give Hugh sixpence."

"We'll see about that when the time comes. Suppose you go and help Hugh? He doesn't know how to manage that boat."

"*I* know! He's very little still." And Roddy went cheerfully to take up his duties as an uncle.

Rosamund and Benedicta looked at one another and smiled at Nanny. Then they went back to the rose-garden, to have a talk with Geoffrey.

CHAPTER XII

CRICKET AT THE MANOR

SIR KENNETH MARCHWOOD did not need to be amused. He was a busy man, with many public duties as Lord of the Manor and with a large estate to look after. But he welcomed joyfully the chance of his favourite pastime, talking about Kenya, and Brian Grandison found himself feeling thoroughly at home from the first moment.

"Come and quarrel with me about Kenya v. Rhodesia," Ken said cheerfully. "I hear you came home by the east coast and called at Mombasa. I hope you went up to Nairobi?"

Jen left them to it and went to the nursery to give the new baby, Barbara Rose, her tea.

Benedicta, arriving home about six, was seized by Jen and Mary-Dorothy and bidden to tell the story of Roddy as an uncle. Rachel had not been warned by telephone that the secret was out, but she and Damaris were keenly interested. Benedicta, sitting enthroned on the topmost grey slab of Windermere beside the bird-bath, and nursing Golden Rory, had an appreciative audience, as she told of Roddy's heart-whole acceptance of the situation and his enthusiasm over the idea of himself as uncle to "all the little children."

"I don't wonder poor Agatha giggled," Jen said. "Nanny was a heroine not to collapse, too."

"I'm thankful for Rosamund's sake. She had been dreading the telling," Mary said.

They asked many questions and managed to draw almost the entire conversation from Benedicta. "You've remembered it all marvellously, Blessing," Jen said. "I'm going right now to phone Ros and congratulate her. Then I want some of you girls to come along to us for cricket. The twins and Jansy are coming, and Kenneth and Brian will play; they're very much amused, and Brian says he's quite out of practice and he expects Brownie will bowl him first ball. He's very taken with her, and he calls her Brownie all the time. I have to keep on saying 'Rosemary!' or she'll forget her real name. He's a good sort, and he's willing to sacrifice himself to help her and the twins to improve their game. Ken and I are always ready for cricket! If some of you would come, we could have quite a good time."

"Ray's first class as a fielder," Damaris said. "She used to make marvellous catches at school. She'll need a little brushing up, but you'll find her quite useful. I'd better not. Suppose I sprained an ankle or broke a leg! Think what Madame would say!"

"Or Sir Bob," Rachel agreed. "You'd better stick to your garden; it's been neglected all day. I'd enjoy a game, Lady Jen."

"I'm not much good, but I'd like to play," Benedicta said.

"We really must help our school people," Jen urged. "Jansy is very keen to see the twins in the junior eleven; there seems no doubt about Margaret, but Elizabeth needs some attention. She mustn't be left out. There isn't much home-work during the summer, so Jansy has decided to work up the twins in earnest. And Rosemary can do with a lot of improvement. We must all join forces and help Jansy."

"And you're glad of the excuse for a game," Mary commented.

"I was a noted bowler in my time," Jen said haughtily. "I'm sure it will come back, with practice. I mean to coach our crowd till all four become famous in the school."

"Will Queen Lavender play?" Rachel asked.

"She smiled and begged to be excused. She'll come sometimes, but she wants the evenings for music. She doesn't get enough time for it," Mary explained.

It was a disappointment to Brian that Mary Damayris held back from the practice games, but he owned that she was right. He offered the use of his car, to take her to Oxford, as soon as her orders arrived from Sir Bob, and Damaris accepted his help joyfully.

"I shall miss you, when you go back to town," she proclaimed.

"You mean you'll miss my car. I'm not going back for a few days," he told her. "My people are having a holiday in Holland, and then they talk of going on to Norway and Sweden. They've

planned to do it for some time; my dad has
Swedish friends, musical folk who want to
entertain him. They're trying to persuade Sir
Ivor and Lady Quellyn to do the tour with them.
Kenneth insists that I'm to stay with him; we
haven't nearly settled the question of Kenya v.
Rhodesia, and Brownie's cricket needs attention
badly."

"I don't care how or where you stay, so long as
you'll take me to Oxford," Damaris declared.

"Oxford is a beautiful and interesting city,"
he said primly. "I shall go to see the colleges
while you are busy, and then I'll bring you
home again. But I shall expect payment for my
services."

She shot a quick wary look at him. "What
payment?"

"Stalls for myself and my people for your
first performance. It will be a great occasion."

"You shall have them," Damaris promised.

He heard the note of relief in her voice and
smiled inwardly. "There won't be any vacant
seats. People will fight for tickets. I'm glad to
know ours are secure."

"It won't be for ages yet. I've a lot of work to
do. But I'm getting on. I can feel it myself, all
the time."

"Good!" Brian said heartily. "Anything I
can do to help will be done. I want to see that
Goose-girl."

On the cricket field at the Manor he met the
rest of the schoolgirls, who lived at the Hall;

D.F.A.   G

Rosemary's twin cousins, Elizabeth and Margaret Marchwood, who had bobbed dark red curls, and were now thirteen; and Jansy Raymond, their cousin, who was fourteen and a half, and was very like them, with the same beautiful red hair, worn in two plaits which were growing so long that she looped them up for cricket, or tied them with a bow on top of her head. Jansy had been May-Queen the previous year and was a person of importance at school.

The reigning Queen, Rosalind, the Lavender Queen, was a tall girl of eighteen, with yellow hair in long plaits which were coiled over her ears for her cookery lessons and were shortly to stay there altogether. She came to watch the cricket and played once or twice, but her heart was with her violin and she could not take any games seriously, though she played tennis occasionally when urged to it by Mary-Dorothy.

A few days after her visit to Kentisbury, Benedicta rang up the castle and asked if Roddy was contented with his position as an uncle.

"He's really rather nice," Rosamund told her. "He's still much amused and he definitely tries to take care of Hugh and help him. He has kept the secret, as he calls it, very carefully. But if I'm at home he comes to me for half an hour, when Hugh has gone to bed, and we have a short while to ourselves, and then he calls me 'Big Sister.' His favourite game is to talk about the little house where we lived together and to pretend we are still there; he's never tired of asking questions about it. I'm going to take him to see it some day; it isn't far away."

"He'll like that. You're being a lovely sister to him, Lady Kentisbury."

Rosamund laughed. "The other night we had people coming to dinner, so I dressed before I sent for Roddy. I was wearing the sapphires that were my wedding present from Joy and the rest of the clan, and when Roddy saw me, he shouted: 'Here's a fine Big Sister!' I said: 'But you've seen me dressed for dinner before, Roddy?' And he said: 'Yes, but you weren't mine then.' He really does feel I belong to him in a very special way. It's quite wonderful."

"Simply marvellous," Benedicta agreed. "It was the way you put it to him."

"He never forgets; he's very careful. He calls me Mother, except during our few special minutes together; but he gives me a funny little grin, as he says it. If the children were older they'd notice, but they are still babies. Roddy quite definitely feels that he and I and Daddy share a secret. Geoffrey's delighted with the whole affair. He has always talked of ' Our boys,' without making any difference, but he means it more than ever now. There's a real understanding friendship between them. Well, good-bye! Give my love to everybody!"

When no cricket was planned, Brian made his way to the Abbey garden, if he could escape from Kenneth. "You're to instruct me about rock gardens," he said, the first time he went.

"Blessing must do that," Damaris informed him. "She's trained; I'm only an amateur. I have luck with the things I stick in, but I don't know why. They like me and so they grow; but it's just luck. Now Blessing knows; she says: 'Don't put that over there, Damson; it wants shade.' Or: 'Put these close to the water, Boss.' Or: 'That thing must have all the sun it can get.' She keeps me straight. She'll teach you."

Rachel, who had come out with Brian, glanced at him, to see if he would show any sign of annoyance.

But his response was apparently sincere. "I'll be delighted to learn from our Blessing! Come and name these rock-plants for me, Benedicta. I'm going to make a list of those I want to have."

"They're mostly sedums, of one sort or another," and Benedicta took charge of his education, while Damaris, whistling gaily, went off to burn her rubbish.

To Jen's delight, the twist in her bowling, which had brought her fame in her schooldays, came back with practice, and to her still greater delight she found she could pass it on to the girls. Margaret in particular was an apt pupil, and her skill was recognised joyfully at school, where she soon took an important place in the team.

"But Rosemary's best at it," Jansy said judicially. "We can all do it a bit, but she's going to be just like you, Aunty Jen. Some of the old girls were watching us at the nets yesterday, and I put Rosemary on to bowl to Elizabeth. They asked

who was the little kid and said she reminded
them of Jen Robins. Myonie piped up and said
Rosemary's mother was called Lady Jen, and I
said she was Rosemary Marchwood, from the
Manor. They just shrieked; they said she couldn't
be your girl, and I said she was. So they said she
wasn't in the least like you, except in her bowling,
and there she was you, all over again; and we
must put her in the team as soon as she's old
enough. I said we'd do that all right and they
needn't worry. Rosemary was pleased; she doesn't
mind not being like you to look at so long as she
can bowl like you."

"Rosemary and Katharine are the only March-
woods in the family," Jen said. "We're very
proud of them. All the boys, and Barbara, are
like me. I'm glad my two big girls are darkies."

"Brownie's going to be a champion bowler.
She very nearly got me out again this evening,"
said Brian, who had been listening.

"I'm going to tell Marigold about our cricket,"
Jansy announced. "It's the sort of thing she'll
want to know."

"And who is Marigold?" Brian asked. "Have I
seen her?"

Everyone crowded round and told him who
Marigold was. "A Queen before Jansy—the
Marigold Queen. In Ceylon, helping her mother
with the babies—Cecily Rose and Jantyjoy. She'll
come back some day—you'll see her—her name's
Joan Fraser, but we call her Littlejan."

"Marigold is a very important person," Jen

assured him. "She came here to school and was one of us for three years. She has a Queen's orange train waiting for her at the Hall and a chestnut pony at Kentisbury. Everything that happens has to be told to Littlejan Fraser. I'm sure she has heard all about you by this time."

"Oh, yes! I told her about him." Jansy grinned at Brian.

"I hope you told the lady only nice things," he said, in mock anxiety.

"Quite nice, I think. But she's not a lady—not that sort of lady—not yet. She's only a girl," Jansy explained.

CHAPTER XIII

WHAT MISS NIGGER FOUND

"YOU'D BETTER remove yourself to the Abbey," Jen said to Brian, on Saturday afternoon. "I'm having a mothers' tea-party. You'd be quite out of place."

"Thanks for the excuse. I like the Abbey and its girls! But what about Kenneth?" Brian asked.

"He must stay and be polite, poor lamb, but there's no need to sacrifice you. It's a party for Rosemary's friend, Hermione Rose, and her mother."

"Myonie?" Brian smiled. "Won't her dad come too?"

"Myonie lost her daddy three months ago," Jen said, suddenly grave. "That's why I don't want too many men about. All our crowd, who knew Mrs. Manley at school, will come, but I've told them not to bring their husbands. It would be so hard on the poor girl. And they've refused to bring any babies; they say it will be quite enough for Myonie and her mother to meet my six and the crowd from the Hall."

"It will be a large party, without any more from outside, and without your two big sons, in whom I don't really believe," Brian said seriously.

"You must come in the holidays and see our boys. Off you go and enjoy yourself!—I say, Brian!"

"Yes, Lady Jen?"

"Which of the girls at the Abbey is it you go to see?"

"Blessing," he said frankly.

"I don't believe it. But if it's Mary Damayris, take care. She won't marry, you know."

"Not yet," he agreed. "But she might, some day." And he went off to ask more questions about rock gardens.

Joy was still away, touring Holland and Scandinavia with her husband and Brian's parents, but Joan, Maidlin, and Rosamund came eagerly to meet Queen Clover. They had, however, decided that their babies would be lost in the tribe of children at the Manor, and that it would be better for Clover to visit each of them in turn and be introduced to their homes.

"I'll send a car for Myonie Rose and her mother," Rosamund said. "They shall come to us for lunch and see our little crowd; then Joan shall call for them and take them to inspect Jenny and Jimmy and Jillian; and they can have tea with Maid and see Marjory and Dorothy and Paul. Much better than meeting the whole lot at once!"

And Jen, after some demur, had agreed, promising to collect Joy's big twins and the three babies to have tea in the garden with Rosemary and Hermione.

"Rosemary will be hostess to quite a large enough party without a dozen more of ours," the Countess said.

Maidlin excused herself as soon as tea was over, begging to be allowed to go to the Abbey.

"I want to congratulate Damaris and hear her plans. I'm sure Clover will forgive me. I'm not often here, and it's a chance to talk to my cousins," she explained to Mrs. Manley. "Kenneth will run me round to the Abbey gate, and Joan will pick me up when she's ready to go home." For they had come together in Joan's car.

"I want to see the girls, too," Joan said. "You run along and have your chat with Mary Damayris, and presently the rest of us will come. Clover and Hermione must see the Abbey."

Benedicta, coming out from tea in the Abbey rooms, met Maidlin at the door. With a word of greeting—"Hallo, Maid! Nice to see you again! Twins and Jackie-Paul all right?"—she turned back into the parlour and seized Brian by the arm.

"Maidlin wants to talk to these two. We'll be in the way. Come along with me!"

"I feel dazed," he complained, as they reached the garden. "Why am I thrust out like this?"

"Because Mrs. Robertson has come on purpose to see the other two. We mustn't butt in. Rachel and Damaris are her cousins. I love her; she was most frightfully kind to me once. But she doesn't want us to-day. You know who she is, don't you? Maidlin di Ravarati, the singer; but she's Mrs. Robertson now. I expect you've heard her on the wireless. I'm going to the farm, to ask Mr. Edwards about the pea-sticks Damaris wants. You'd better come with me."

"Somebody else means to come, too," said Brian, much amused by the way first one part of the family and then another told him he was not wanted.

The black kitten, Miss Nigger, was prancing ahead, her bushy tail erect, quite obviously intending to go to the farm with them.

"She has friends there. We're going to begin calling her Mrs. Nigger quite soon," Benedicta said grimly. "We must be sure to bring her back; she'd rather like to stay at the farm altogether. Rory won't come; he despises Miss Nigger's little ways."

She did her business with the farmer and then looked round for Miss Nigger.

"She's having a drink," Brian remarked.

"Out of that round stone basin. I've often thought it would make a good bird-bath for the garden. We could do with another," Benedicta said. "Come and look at it; it's a perfect circle. I believe it's quite old."

Brian looked down at the stone bowl, from which Miss, or Mrs. Nigger, was refreshing herself. "It's rather a jolly thing. Would the man give it to you?"

"I should think so. It looks as if it had lain there for centuries. I've seen the puppies drinking out of it."

Benedicta knelt to examine the bowl more

closely. "There are marks on it. How odd! Could it be—oh, Brian! Could it be anything that mattered? Something from the Abbey, put out here and forgotten? It has carving round the edge. I believe it means something. Brian, what have we found?"

Brian was on his knees, too, scanning the carved edges of the basin. "There are small figures, much broken, but I can see them. They have wings. I believe they're angels."

For one moment he and Benedicta stared at one another across the round stone bowl.

"It must be part of the Abbey! Oh, come and tell Rachel!" Benedicta leapt to her feet and raced to the gap in the hedge and across the garden. Brian caught up the indignant Miss Nigger and ran after her, and was in time to hear her cry, as she burst into the parlour:

"Oh, Rachel, come! In the farmyard—come and look! That old round drinking-trough; it has angels carved on it! Could it—oh, could it be—do you think it could possibly be—the old font, from the Abbey church?"

The conference broke up in wild excitement. Rachel, holding her white gown, raced across the garden, with Damaris and Maidlin just behind. Benedicta dashed after them, and Brian, amused but deeply thrilled, stopped only to thrust Miss Nigger into the room and close the door on her. Then, leaving her protesting loudly that it had been her discovery and she was still thirsty, he ran after the girls.

They were on their knees by the puppies' drinking-bowl, tracing the half-defaced figures on the edge with eager reverent fingers.

"I've seen the thing a million times, but I've never looked at it properly," Damaris cried.

Rachel pushed away the nettles that grew round the bowl. "Look!" she said gently. "Maid, look here! Two babies' heads; are they cherubs, or just the babies who were brought to the church? It is the old font; it must be. Oh, Maid, what a find!"

"How wonderful!" Maidlin whispered, deeply moved. "The font from the church, after four hundred years! It's a holy thing; it must go back to the Abbey. And we must tell Joan. What a treasure! How did you find out, Benedicta?"

"Miss Nigger was having a drink. Brian and I came to look. Do you really think it's the font, Maid?"

"It looks like it to me. Angels and babies, on a round stone basin. It must have stood on a pedestal——"

"There are broken bits of stone among these nettles." Damaris had seized a stick and was slashing the weeds aside. "It's in pieces, but I believe—well, there's carving here too."

"What's all this? What's going on here?" Mr. Edwards from the farm was standing above them.

Rachel explained in a few quick words. "This old stone trough is carved with angels and other figures. We think it may be the font from the Abbey church."

"And we think these stones are bits of the pillar it stood on," Damaris added.

"Well, now, I never did! Let's see!" and Mr. Edwards lifted the broken lumps of stone and laid them on the path.

With careful hands the girls examined them.

"There's a snake here," Damaris asserted. "Crawling up, but it's broken off. Has anybody any more of my snake?"

"Yes, here's the head," Benedicta cried. "Would they have a snake on a font?"

"A serpent," Rachel corrected her. "I think they might."

"Creeping up to seize the baby before it was safely baptised," Damaris grinned. "But would they have infants in the monks' church?"

"Joan says part of it was used as the parish church," Maidlin explained. "The village church was built about sixteen hundred. Before that the villagers came to the Abbey church. Girls, I'm sure of it. It is the old font. How glad Joan will be! She's coming here presently. What news for her!"

"You've given a treasure to the Abbey, Blessing," Rachel said.

"It was Miss Nigger," Benedicta said honestly. "And Brian helped."

"You belong to the Abbey, now that you've found something for it," Damaris told Brian.

"I'm overjoyed to belong, but I really didn't do anything except discover the angels on the edge," he confessed.

"Ahoy! Where's everybody?" A united shout came from the garden. Jen and Rosamund and Joan together could make themselves heard very thoroughly.

"They've come! We must tell them!" Rachel and Maidlin, Damaris and Benedicta, disappeared in a wild rush back to the garden.

CHAPTER XIV

A TREASURE FOR THE ABBEY

BRIAN LOOKED at John Edwards. "You'll have the whole crowd here in a moment. You'll give them the font, if it is the font, won't you? Would you let me——?"

"They shall have it. Nay, I want nothing for it, sir. 'Tis theirs by rights. It must go back to the Abbey, for sure. To think of it! That old trough that our pups have drunk out of for hundreds of years! And nobody looking at it close-like!"

"You need to look closely to see that there is anything special about it," Brian assented.

"My grandfather used them Abbey rooms for the farm," John Edwards explained. "Store-rooms and stables they were, for centuries, till old Sir Antony from the Hall took over the place and set it to rights and turned it into an Abbey again. Like enough this is the font, and it was picked up and brought here long ago."

"Miss ' Blessing ' suggested using it as a bird-bath. She was going to ask you for it," Brian laughed.

"Aye, well, it would make a good one. Can these be put together, I wonder? Nay, I think not; there's too much missing." John was examining the scraps of the pedestal. "They'll need to give it a new stool to stand on."

Through the gap in the hedge came the party from the Manor, Jen leading, Rosamund a close second; Joan, quieter but radiant, was not far behind. They knelt in an excited group around the font, Maidlin eagerly showing the angels, the babies' heads, the crawling serpent.

Damaris tried to put the pieces of the pedestal together, and Benedicta searched among the nettles for more fragments of stone.

Rachel, used to looking after tourists, saw strangers by the hedge and went to investigate. "Did you come to see the Abbey?"

"We came with Joan and Jen and Rosamund," Clover Manley explained. "But they all ran away."

"You must be Myonie's mother, and this must be Hermione," Rachel smiled. "Where is Rosemary?"

"She was coming with us, but the twin boys fell down and she stayed to comfort them. What has happened?"

Rachel told of the great find. "They'll remember you presently. They're all thrilled to the limit."

"It is the font. I'm certain of it," Joan was saying. "It must come back to the Abbey. Mr. Edwards will give it to us, I'm sure."

"'Tis yours, ma'am—Mrs. Raymond, I should say—and I'm right glad you should have it."

"That's nice of you." Joan smiled up at him.

"We'll find another drinking bowl for the puppies."

"They shall have a beauty, of Sussex pottery, from Kentisbury," Rosamund promised. "What will you do with your new treasure, Joan?"

"You could have the pedestal rebuilt, using the old stones, and stand it in the middle of the garth," Damaris said.

"And it would look just like a bird-bath," Joan retorted. "That won't do. Try again, somebody!"

"They'd want to dance ' Sellenger's ' round it, Damson," Benedicta hinted.

"What about putting it out on the site of the church, somewhere near where it used to stand? But I'm afraid it would still suggest a bird-bath," Rosamund said.

"And we'd still want to use it as a maypole. Better not put temptation in our way. Keep it in the refectory, with the other Abbey treasures," Jen suggested.

"A font in a refectory, Jenny-Wren?" Joan looked doubtful.

"There's only one place," Maidlin began, her eyes dreamy.

Everybody looked at her. Brian, in particular, was interested, for he had had no time to see her properly since Benedicta had told him who she was. Small and slight, with very dark eyes, and black hair coiled on her neck, she was as Italian in looks as her first name had been. He hoped some day he would hear her sing; he had often heard of her from his father.

She started and coloured, as the others turned to her expectantly. "I oughtn't to have said it. Joan must decide."

"But I'd like to know what you would do, Maidie?" Joan coaxed.

"It should stand in the sacristy." Maidlin gazed at her dreamily. "That's the only part of the church we have left."

"The vestry! That's a good idea!" Jen and Rosamund spoke together. "Well done, Maid!"

"There's nothing in there, except the rose window and some coloured tiles," Maidlin went on. "It would be something for Rachel to show to visitors in the sacristy." And she gave Rachel a smile of understanding friendship.

"I like that idea," Rachel exclaimed. "I've always loved the sacristy."

"As near to the original church as we can put it," Joan agreed. "You're right, Maidie dear; the sacristy is the place. We'll send for the expert from town who comes regularly to inspect the Abbey, and he shall decide which of the old stones can be used for the pedestal and build it for us, with some new ones added. We can't waste that charming serpent! Benedicta, I do thank you very much indeed. This is a great gift for the Abbey!"

"I'm going to ring 'Welcome Home! Glad to see you!' for the font!" Damaris cried, and rushed off in excitement to the garth.

"You ought really to thank Miss Nigger,"

Benedicta said again. "Where is she, I wonder? She'll be doing something she shouldn't."

"I shut her in your parlour," Brian said.

"Then she's on the table, spilling things and stuffing herself with milk. We'd better go to the rescue!" Benedicta cried, and raced after Damaris, followed by Brian.

"Perhaps I can help. It seems to be my fault, but I meant well," he apologised.

As the sound of the Abbey bells rang out, Joan went to Clover Manley. "Do forgive us! Sometimes we find a new treasure for the Abbey and it goes to our heads. Come and see it! The carving is defaced and incomplete, but the angels and babies are quite recognisable. Don't you want to see them, Myonie?"

"I'd like Brownie to show me, please." Hermione was still shy with all these new friends.

"Brownie hasn't seen it herself yet. You'll be able to show her," Joan smiled.

"Brownie must have seen it often, as we've all done, but she didn't know what it was," Rachel said.

Clover Manley, whose real name was Anne, was a small brown-haired girl who had looked very pretty as a Queen, when she had worn a train of dull pink ornamented with green four-leaved clovers. She came eagerly to see the font; then she and Myonie went with Joan to tour the ruins, and Maidlin followed Damaris to hear more about her plans.

A flight of schoolgirls swooped from the

tresaunt out on to the garth; the red-haired
twins and Jansy leading, Rosemary and Queen
Lavender behind. "What are the bells for? Who's
come?" they shouted.

"'Welcome home. Glad to see you!' Who is it,
Mary Damayris?" The twins knew the code by
heart.

Damaris turned from the bells. "Ask the Abbey
Guide! She's there, in the garden."

The crowd swept out to surround Rachel, who
led them to the farm to see the new treasure.

CHAPTER XV

AMBROSE AGAIN

THE SCHOOLGIRLS were still exclaiming in delight over the angels and the serpent when John Edwards, who had disappeared into the farmhouse, came hurrying back. "Mrs. Raymond? Has she gone home?"

"Not yet. She's taking friends round the Abbey." Rachel, with one look at his face, turned to go with him, leaving the girls still busy.

"I must tell her. It'll please her, sure enough," John Edwards said mysteriously.

They met Joan, Jen and Rosamund on the garth. Maidlin and Damaris saw the farmer's face as he passed through the cloisters, and with a look at one another they followed Rachel quickly.

"Something up," Damaris murmured. "John's bursting with news!"

"Something more?" Maidlin cried.

"Mrs. Raymond, ma'am, I asked my grandmother if she——"

"His grandmother?" Maidlin asked incredulously.

Damaris nodded. "She'll be a hundred, if she

lives till Christmas. A regular old witch, who never goes out. But she's hale and hearty, and——"

"Oh, listen! Hear what he's telling Joan! His grandmother can wait!"

"If she remembered that old trough, and she laughed right out, and said it was the pup-trough, and her granddad told her his granddad had said he'd been told by his father that the Old One who lived in the gate-house had put it there, and when the pups and birds drank out of it he said: ' Let the small ones drink. 'Tis good that they should use it.'"

"Ambrose!" Jen gave a shout of joy.

"The Old One who lived in the gate-house was Ambrose, the lay-brother, who saved so many things for us," Joan said quickly, to Mrs. Manley. "We'll tell you his story later. Oh, Mr. Edwards, that's splendid! Will you please thank your grandmother very much?"

"It goes back a long way, with all those grand-fathers," Rosamund said. "There evidently was a family tradition about Ambrose. Why didn't the old lady tell you before, Mr. Edwards?"

"I said that to her, my lady, and she said nobody ever asked her about the pup-trough."

"How very true!" Rosamund admitted. "Why should anyone ask about a pup-trough?"

"I'm surprised that Ambrose wasn't shocked to see the dogs and birds using the font," Jen began.

"Perhaps he felt that by using it they would disguise the fact that it was the font and so save it from harm, if any of the King's men came back to add to the destruction of the Abbey," Joan suggested.

"Ambrose was very sensible. I expect that was it." Jen sounded relieved. "Dear old chap! What heaps of treasures we owe to him!"

"And I dare say he became tolerant and broad-minded in his old age," Joan added. "Some day I'd like to see your old lady, Mr. Edwards. Would she talk to me?"

"She would that, ma'am. But she's going on for her hundred. Best come soon!"

"Yes, I mustn't put it off too long. She's quite a link with the old days. Rachel!" Joan called to her Abbey Guardian. "When the font is placed on its pillar in the sacristy, if you care to keep it filled with water I won't object. We won't say we're using it as a bird-bath, but the robins may learn to fly in through the rose window for a drink, and it would be a safe place for them, away from your cats! The Abbey must be hospitable to all who come, even to the sparrows and robins."

"A lovely idea!" Rachel said warmly. "I'll always keep it filled, if I may."

"It will add to your daily work, but you won't grudge a little extra. And since Ambrose didn't mind the small ones using it, we needn't." Joan smiled at her.

"I keep water-bowls for the birds already, in odd corners where they don't show," Rachel confessed. "I'll be glad to fill another for old Ambrose's small ones. I like his name for them!

There's one very faithful robin who is always on the garth. I'm terribly afraid Rory will catch him some day."

"Ambrose was a dear. I'm so glad he is linked with the font," Maidlin said.

"Where's our Blessing all this time? We must tell her about Ambrose," Damaris began. "And what's become of Brian?"

Benedicta appeared at the parlour door. "What's going on? We've had the most awful job, clearing up Miss Nigger's mess. She'd spilt the milk jug and knocked down the butter dish, and there were crumbs all over the floor. Rory had done his share, too. I've cleaned the house, so you can come in for your talk. But they are a wicked pair."

"You really are a Blessing!" Damaris said, with enthusiasm. "Has Brian been helping?"

"He's been a brick. He's all buttery; he did the floor. He's in the bathroom, with a kettle of hot water."

"He's clean now." Brian came to meet them. "It was my fault, but I didn't know a tragedy would happen. I had no idea of the evil lurking in such innocent little people."

"You rather live in our bathroom, don't you?" Damaris mocked. "Oh—Maid! This is Brian Grandison. You know his father's music for my *Rainbow Corner* ballet."

"I hope to see you dance to that fairy music," Brian began.

"I know your father's music, quite apart from

Damaris's ballets," Maidlin said. "I'm glad to
meet you, Mr. Grandison. My husband sent a
special message, in case I saw you; Jen wouldn't
let him come to-day. He wants to meet you, so
we hope you'll come to The Pallant."

"Maid has twin baby girls and a very new boy,"
Damaris said.

"I shall certainly come, Mrs. Robertson. Please
thank Dr. Robertson very warmly for me."

"You'd better be introduced," Damaris said.
"You didn't know what you were doing when you
came to the Abbey! If you meet one of the crowd,
you have to meet the lot. Blessing, take him and
tell him who they all are. Maid and I must have
our talk! She'll be rushing off to Jackie-Paul
before I've told her everything."

Out on the garth Brian was introduced to
"The owner of the Abbey, Mrs. Raymond, but
we call her Mrs. Joan," as Benedicta said; and
to the Countess of Kentisbury.

"We've heard of you, Mr. Grandison. I hope
you'll come to meet my husband," Rosamund
said.

"You'll have to pay a round of visits," Benedicta
warned him.

"Tell these two about Ambrose, Rachel. Clover
and Hermione and I are going round the Abbey,"
Joan said. "You'd better tell the schoolgirls, too.
What a thrilling letter Jansy will have to write to
Littlejan Fraser!"

Rosamund looked at Jen, as Rachel led Brian
and Benedicta back to the garden. "Those two

seem very good friends. Mr. Brian Grandison has made himself completely at home."

"Quite one of the family," Jen agreed. "He's staying with Kenneth and me, but he spends half his time in the Abbey."

"And which of the girls is the attraction? Not Rachel, I hope; the Abbey mustn't lose its Guardian! He seems very pally with young Benedicta."

"I'm afraid it's Mary Damayris, Rosamunda."

"Afraid? They'd make a fine couple!"

"Yes, but would she? Wouldn't she break his heart? She cares for nothing but her dancing."

"She'll have to choose," Rosamund remarked. "It would be worth while giving up even her career for a good man."

"I think so, too, of course, but I don't know if she'll see it that way."

"You're sure it isn't Benedicta he wants? She's a nice child, and quite pretty," Rosamund suggested.

"Certain," Jen said firmly. "He told me to-day that it *is* Blessing, as he calls her. That was quite enough."

"Dear, dear!" Rosamund said. "That's serious. As you say, if he says it's Blessing, it definitely is not. I hope she won't make any mistake about it. We don't want her heart broken, too."

"Blessing's head is screwed on the right way. She knows what she's about. I'm not worried over her heart," Jen said confidently.

CHAPTER XVI

HELP FOR DAMARIS

DAMARIS RECEIVED her orders from Sir Bob within a few days. He gave her the address of the hospital in Oxford where she would have massage and special baths, and told her to see the doctors and make arrangements as to day and time.

"I shall drive you over and bring you back," Brian said.

Rachel turned to him quickly. "But you aren't staying here. We must make other plans."

"I'll ask Lady Jen to lend me her Rover and I'll drive myself," Damaris said defiantly, foreseeing opposition.

"You can't do that," Brian exclaimed.

"Why not? I'm a good driver."

"I'm sure you are. But it wouldn't do." He looked at Rachel.

"The treatment may tire you," Rachel explained. "You mustn't attempt to drive home. That's what you meant?" and she looked at Brian.

"I'm sure it would be unwise," he agreed. "Is there anyone else?"

"I can drive, but I can't leave the Abbey."

"I can't drive," Benedicta said mournfully. "Wish I could! Perhaps I could learn?"

"I shall take Mary Damayris to Oxford to make her plans," Brian said firmly. "After that we'll see what we can do."

"I'd hate to go by train," Damaris acknowledged.

"It won't come to that," he assured her. "Or only for a week or two. When my dad and mother come back from Europe, they're invited to stay with the Quellyns; I heard this morning. If Lady Quellyn will have me too, I shall be able to take you to Oxford."

"That's jolly for them all," Rachel said. "They really have made friends on this trip. But the Hall will be badly overcrowded."

"Then I shall dump myself on Kenneth," Brian said cheerfully. "I won't be left in town alone. And I have to visit all your friends—Jock Robertson, and the Kentisbury people, and Mrs. Raymond and her family."

"You'll need to come back," Damaris said gleefully.

"But what about your house in the north, and your rock-garden?" Benedicta demanded.

"They'll wait for me. We'll all go north in August and inspect my property and make plans. Can you leave your job?" and he looked at Rachel.

"Mrs. Raymond will find somebody for the Abbey; I asked her on Saturday. She says I must go with Damaris," Rachel said quietly.

When Jen Marchwood heard the new plans she acted promptly.

"When Brian leaves us, we'll send you to

Oxford, Dammy-Marry. If Henderson is needed here, I'll drive you myself. I'd enjoy an hour in Oxford."

"Not twice a week!" Rachel protested.

"Once a week, and Henderson can go the other time. He really ought to be taking Rosemary and Mike to Wycombe every day, but he's spared that, as they go with the crowd from the Hall. He can easily run you in once or twice a week. But if Brian is here we'll withdraw in his favour, as he offered first."

"You're fixed up, Marry," Rachel said, in great relief. "It's more than kind of you, Mrs. Brown!"

"I'll do anything for you, when you call me Mrs. Brown!" Jen mocked.

"A most suitable name for the mother of Brownie," Brian remarked.

He drove Damaris to Oxford and was glad to be there to bring her home, for the doctors offered to begin treatment at once, and she found it tiring, as Rachel had foreseen.

"I don't believe I could drive home. You are a boon and a blessing, Brian," she said wearily. "But it's going to be worth it. They say it will help me a lot and they're all thrilled; they're coming in a crowd to see me dance."

"There'll be no seats left for the public. You'll need them all for your friends." He smiled at her. "Don't tire yourself by talking. I can guess how you feel."

Damaris gratefully lapsed into silence, appreciating his understanding. He stopped at a wayside café and made her eat, and she owned to feeling rested by the time they reached home.

He took her to Oxford twice, and then admitted that his parents were returning to London and he ought to join them. On the last day of his visit he drove, by invitation, to Kentisbury, to meet the Earl and his family, and came home delighted with his welcome and with the ancient castle, and full of amusement over the two sets of twin girls, and especially over Roddy.

"A fine sturdy little chap," he reported to the girls in the Abbey. "He looked at me for a time and decided I was to be trusted. So he came to share his secret and tell me he was ' uncle to all those children, but they're too young to understand.' I fancy he has grown a lot in his mind since he heard the news."

"I hope it hasn't aged him too much," Benedicta remarked.

"No, not that. He's a jolly little fellow. But he's not a baby any longer. He's very proud of being ' my lady's little brother.' He told me about it."

"You're fond of children, aren't you?" Rachel commented.

"I've never had much to do with them. I've rather avoided them, till I came here; I was afraid I wouldn't know how to speak to them. But I seem to get on all right with Brownie and Mike and Katharine at the Manor. I'd like to have some of my own one day. Think of having a boy like Roddy, or a little Brownie! But I must go and report to Lady Jen. She wants to hear my impressions of Kentisbury."

"Did you go to see Mrs. Joan?" Rachel asked. "It isn't far from the Castle."

"I came back that way. She has a delightful little family, too, although the elder boy is away at school and the big girl is here, of course."

"Jansy is proud of her brothers and sisters. Come into the Abbey for a moment, before you drive back to the Manor!"

Puzzled, he followed the three girls through the gate to the garth. Then he gave a startled exclamation, for Joan, whom he had left in her home in Sussex with Baby Jillian and the rest, was crossing the green square towards him.

Then he pulled himself together, with a laugh. It was not Joan; instead of the big plaits there was short hair, beautifully waved, of the same rich dark red.

"What an amazing likeness! I quite thought it was Mrs. Raymond!"

"We knew you would," Rachel agreed, while the other two laughed. "But you've seen Jansy and the twins, and you know they are only cousins, although they're so much alike. You should have guessed. Lady Joy, here is Brian—Mr. Grandison."

"I'm glad to meet you, Mr. Grandison," Joy said. "I've been seeing that beautiful font; I hear you had a hand in finding it. It looks as much at home as if it had stood in the sacristy since

Ambrose's day, instead of being used by the farm puppies for centuries. And the sparrows and robins are flying in and out of my beloved rose window as if there had always been a drink for them there. I surprised two being busy and happy; a very pretty sight! I've a message from your people. Ivor and I had to come home direct from Stockholm, as he has a concert on Saturday, but your mother and father have returned to Amsterdam for a week more with the friends there. You won't want to be at home alone, so perhaps you'll come to us, or stay on at the Manor?"

"That's very kind. I must consult my present hostess, but I'll gladly take advantage of your offer, if Lady Jen wants to get rid of me."

"She won't let you go," Rachel said.

"You'll be able to take me to Oxford again," Damaris exulted.

"If Jen holds on to you, you must dine with us and meet my husband," Joy said. "You are coming to the Hall with your people later, so we must get to know you."

Her pleasure in this ripening friendship with the composer, John Grant Grandison, was obvious. A writer of songs herself, some of them charming and all very pleasant, she had welcomed the chance of the trip to Amsterdam in such company, and had been overjoyed when the journey to Stockholm was proposed. She liked Mrs. Grandison and she admired the composer; a fortnight's travelling together would do much to turn their acquaintance into friendship. All had worked out as she had hoped; she was shortly to entertain the great man in her own home, and she was prepared to be very gracious to his son.

Brian offered to run her round to her own gate and up the long beech avenue, but Joy laughed and declined with thanks. "I'll walk through the garden. I must go back; the school crowd will be arriving soon and there will be shrieks of excitement from the twins. They don't expect me till to-morrow, but we managed to save a day on the journey. I'll ring Jen and ask if I may have you for a few days, Mr. Grandison."

"Now you really have met everybody," Damaris said, as they escorted Joy to the Abbey gate and then turned back to the garth. "Lady Jen won't let you go. Will you really take me to Oxford next week? I'll love you for ever!"

Rachel looked at Brian quickly.

"That's bribery," he said. "I'll take you, Mary Damayris."

"You know I didn't mean anything," she said hurriedly.

"I know it only too well," he retorted.

"Marry, you mustn't say such things to Brian!" Rachel remonstrated that night.

"He knows. Don't be daft, Ray! Don't imagine things!"

Rachel said no more. If Damaris could really think she was romancing about Brian's feelings, then it was too soon to awaken her. But did Damaris think it? Rachel was not at all sure.

She suspected that Damaris knew very well, but that she was fighting against the knowledge.

"Perhaps he is teaching her, in his own way. I must wait," Rachel said to herself.

CHAPTER XVII

A MUSICAL EVENING

THE SUMMER term went on its way. Queen Lavender reigned quietly and happily over the Hamlet Club, enjoying her music, and working a little, but not too hard, at her cookery. Jansy, with exams ahead, did well in cricket but was too busy to play in matches. The twins, in the junior team, both distinguished themselves, and, to their amusement, seemed likely to make their names as cricketers and not as musicians, as they had expected. But they practised with the orchestra regularly and were considered useful, Elizabeth with her 'cello, Margaret with her fiddle; and Lavender, as first violin, watched them and gave them hints at home.

Rosemary's friendship with Myonie deepened and seemed likely to be lasting, and Jen was glad, for Hermione and her mother were lonely people now, and through the school friendship she saw a chance to help Clover and bring companionship and pleasure into her quiet life. There were many invitations for Myonie and her mother, to the Manor, the Castle, the Pallant, and the Hall; Rosamund insisted that she was an unofficial godmother and always called Hermione "Myonie Rose."

Little Michael enjoyed school so much that Katharine, at four and a half, clamoured to be allowed to go too. But Jen begged her to wait a little longer and pointed out what a great help she could be with Chris and Barney; and Katharine, much flattered, consented to be the big girl who helped her mother at home.

Damaris went regularly to Oxford and found the treatment definitely helpful. By July she admitted that Sir Bob had been right and that this waiting time had made all the difference. She was more loose and supple, and in every way she was growing stronger.

Brian stayed at the Manor and then went home to join his parents. Presently they all came to the Hall, and while Joy and Ivor rejoiced in their guests, he spent his time in the Abbey or in the garden, being instructed by Damaris and Benedicta in the ways of rock plants. The crimson sedums flowered on Windermere's grey blocks; Wirral's red slabs of stone were gay with yellow rock roses. He was enthusiastic over them all and made many notes for his home among the Lakes.

John Grant Grandison was a great friend of Mary Damayris. In the old days she and Rachel had invited him to tea and had told him all about the new ballet Damaris wished to make; he had written fascinating music for her dances and had shared in her success. He came to the Abbey to congratulate her on her recovery and to promise new music for future work. His wife, who had

met the girls in town, came too, to see the garden
of which Brian had said so much; and her eyes
rested on Damaris thoughtfully, as if she tried to
read what lay ahead for them all.

They returned to town in due course, but Brian
found no difficulty in making excuses to run down
to the Manor, bringing friends from Africa to
meet Kenneth or to see the Abbey. He was often
in the garden with Damaris and Benedicta, and
Rachel watched and waited, but said nothing to
disturb the carefree friendship.

Towards the end of July, Joy and Ivor gave a
musical evening for their friends. The Grandisons
were invited to stay the night: Jock Robertson
brought his wife and his viola, and Maidlin sang
several of Joy's songs.

Queen Lavender, who was really Rosalind Kane
and Rosamund's niece, played a violin sonata by
Vivaldi, and Ivor Quellyn, accompanying her on
the piano, glanced significantly at Jock Robertson,
with thoughts of future concerts in his mind.

Lindy Bellanne, who had come with Maidlin,
sang a soprano "lark" song, full of trills and
laughter, and again Ivor looked at Jock.

"How that child's voice has improved, since
she was in America with us! You've done wonders
with her."

"She's nearly ready for her first concert," Jock
assented. "She has worked well, and her voice is
quite out of the ordinary run."

At Mrs. Grandison's urgent request, Elizabeth
and Margaret played together, with their mother

at the piano. Joy would not have suggested that they should play, but the guests had heard of the trios she had written and begged that they might hear one of them.

Joan and Rosamund and their husbands were the appreciative audience, as Joan said, along with the three girls from the Abbey, who had been urged to come, and had unearthed what Rachel called "town frocks" for the occasion. Rosamund wore the sapphires which had been her wedding gift from the family and looked, as Roddy would have said: "A fine big sister." She was very well this summer, with a contented light in her eyes and no trace of the wistfulness which had been there for the last year. She and Geoffrey had a happy secret, which only Maidlin shared so far, though the rest of her circle guessed and rejoiced with them.

But the evening was not wholly given up to music. In the big hall, with its stained glass windows catching the last sunset light and throwing coloured gleams on the polished floor, the old oak tables and settles were pushed to the walls by Jock and Kenneth, and Rosalind played the haunting music of "Hunsdon House," while Joy and Jen, Joan and Jansy, Rosamund and Maidlin, Elizabeth and Margaret, walked through the stately movements of the square for eight.

"But that's not a country dance! It's more like a minuet," Brian protested.

"A court dance, in the old days, I imagine," Joy said. "We aren't dressed for real country dances, but we might manage 'Newcastle', just to show you the difference."

Jen, with a laugh in the direction of the great composer, produced her wooden pipe. "Mary-Dorothy can take my place."

Maidlin spoke in a quick undertone to Queen Lavender. "Ask Rosamund if you may dance instead of her! Yes, please, Rosalind! She won't want to do 'Newcastle,' particularly on a polished floor; but she won't care to say so."

Rosalind gave her a startled look. Then, obediently, she went to her aunt. "I'd like to dance, Aunt Rosamund. Do you mind?"

"I'll be delighted," Rosamund said, looking relieved.

"Nanta Rose! With me, Nanta Rose!" cried Jansy.

"Two Queens together. Very suitable, Lob," and Rosamund went to sit with Mrs. Grandison.

The sweet high notes of the pipe delighted Grandison—as everyone called him—and he begged for more. Jen played morris tunes, and insisted that Elizabeth and Margaret should dance "Old Mother Oxford" to her piping, and Jansy "Bacca Pipes," to Rosalind's fiddle. Joan and Joy, after some coaxing, danced a minuet, and Jen told Brian in a rapid undertone how they had done this as schoolgirls and had won the heart of old Sir Antony, Joy's grandfather, and of how he had left the Hall to Joy and the Abbey to Joan.

"Now do 'Princess Royal' for us," she demanded. "You danced that for Sir Antony, too."

Joan shook her head sadly at her. "In these frocks? We should look silly doing capers, Jenny-Wren!"

"I'll dash upstairs and put on Rosalind's school tunic. She's a long person, like me. Then I'll do ' Princess Royal ' for you, *and* ' Lumps of Plum Pudding,'" said the tall mother of eight.

"Oh, please do! I'd love to see you dance in my tunic!" cried Queen Lavender.

"Calm down, Jenny-Wren. All that morris music has gone to your poor little head," Joy said severely. "Kenneth will take you home, if you go on like this."

"Would Mary Damayris dance for us?" asked Mrs. Grandison, and Jen subsided hurriedly.

Damaris rose without hesitation. "Three months ago I'd have said I couldn't. But now— yes, I will, if you really would like it."

Benedicta, with demure eyes, handed her a bag. "Your shoes," she said. "Lady Joy asked me to bring them, just in case they were wanted."

Damaris raised her brows, but made no comment. She changed and then looked up. "What do you want—oh, will you really? That is good of you!"

"The dance of the fairy in the wood," said the composer of the fairy music, who had gone to the piano.

"That music nearly broke my heart one day, when I thought I'd never dance again." Damaris stood by the piano, looking down at him. "I heard it suddenly, by accident, on the wireless, and I just went all to pieces."

He glanced up at her and nodded. "Poor child! But it's all right now?"

"Oh, yes! I'll love to do the fairy dance. And out of that horrible moment came the discovery of a new bit of the Abbey. We'll tell you the story afterwards. We found a treasure."

"Treasure out of tragedy," he said. "Well done!"

He played the opening chords, and Damaris, in the cleared space, began to dance.

Up in the shadows, Joy's two nurses hung over the gallery railing. As former Queens, Striped Queen and Garden Queen, Beatrice and Grace were friends of those below and they knew themselves privileged people. They had been invited to join the party, but had felt shy and had excused themselves, saying they could not leave the children. But they had listened to the music and had watched the morris and country dances. To see Mary Damayris dance was a rare treat.

Rachel, hiding in a corner, shot a look at Brian. Then a real shock went through her, for he was not looking at Damaris. Everyone else had eyes fixed on that lithe whirling figure, so beautiful in every movement, so joyful and radiant; the exulting fairy in the wood. But Brian had turned away. If his eyes were on anyone they were on Benedicta, who stood, unconscious and breathless, watching the dance.

Rachel felt suddenly sick. She had not seen the

quick glance he had thrown at Damaris as the dance began, or she might perhaps have understood. Did he not care even to see Marry? No one could have been more beautiful. What had happened?

Everyone crowded round Damaris, offering congratulations and giving warm thanks. From the shadowy stairs came wild applause, and at Joy's suggestion the twins raced up to the gallery and each seized a nurse and dragged her, protesting and still shy, to be introduced.

Rachel, making her way to Damaris, heard Brian's words. "Thank you, Mary Damayris! Now I know why they call you the little pirouette!" he said.

"But you weren't looking!" Rachel said to herself, puzzled and hurt.

"It wasn't because they liked my pirouettes," Damaris remonstrated. "It was because I would put them in where nobody expected them. I could hear them in the music, but no one else could. I got into fearful trouble; I was kicked out of the ballet. Martin Bernard never forgot; he always teases me about it."

"But they found they couldn't do without you." Grandison smiled at her.

"I want to take Damaris home, if Lady Joy will excuse us now," Rachel said. "She has Oxford to-morrow; she'll be too tired."

"Very true," Brian agreed. "I'll see you all safely to the Abbey."

Damaris and Benedicta hooted derisively, but

he held to his purpose. He was silent, however, and bade them good night abruptly as they reached the Abbey gate, and turned to go back through the garden.

Damaris chuckled. "What's the matter with him? He's forgotten that Blessing doesn't live with us! If he wanted to see anybody home he should have taken her down that dark lane to the village!"

"I don't need anyone. I've gone alone hundreds of times in the dark."

"Got your torch?"

Benedicta flashed it on. "Good night!"

"Sure you'll be all right? We'll both come, if you like," Rachel said.

"Not a scrap of need. It's only a step. Put Damson to bed. She needs it, after giving us that treat. Thanks, Boss! You're lovely when you dance."

"Run along to bed, child!" said Damaris.

CHAPTER XVIII

SISTER RACHEL

DAMARIS SWITCHED on the light under the crimson shade. The two cats lay curled up on the couch; the black one opened an eye and flicked her tail in welcome, but Golden Rory sprang down at once and came shouting his greeting to Rachel.

For once she had no time for cats. She patted him briefly, but turned to Damaris.

"Marry!" The word fairly shot from her. "Whom does Brian come here to see?"

Damaris stared at her. "What do you mean? What's the matter?"

"I must know. He wouldn't look at your dance. Why?"

"*I* don't know! I saw him look the other way. I don't usually think about people when I'm dancing, but I did notice that." Damaris stood looking down and playing with the roses on the table. "Ray, what's up?"

"I was sure he came to see you. To-night I thought it might be a mistake."

"I hope it is a mistake!" Damaris broke out. "I don't want that sort of thing; not for ages yet."

"It might be Benedicta," Rachel began.

Damaris swung round, her face ablaze with

indignation. "Benedicta? Are you mad? *Bene-dicta!*"

"Why not? They're very good friends, and she looked really pretty to-night. That white frock made her hair much yellower than usual. She's a jolly girl."

"She's only a kid," Damaris cried. "And anyway, Brian comes to see *me*! Benedicta! What utter rot!"

And she was gone, whirling into her inner room and slamming the door.

Rachel, looking grave, took off her frock and slipped on her dressing-gown. She prepared supper for the cats and gave one moment to Rory, loving him and pulling his ears. Then she poured milk into a pan and put biscuits on a tray. Marry was always hungry after dancing.

Suddenly Damaris flung open her door. "Ray! Ray, I want you!"

Rachel was beside her in an instant, on her knees by the bed, where Damaris had thrown herself. "Marry dear, can I help?"

"Do you really think he comes for Benedicta?" Damaris whispered, her face hidden.

"I always thought he came to see you. But to-night he seemed different, and I was worried."

"It isn't you?"

"Oh, no! I like him a lot, but not in that way. But, Marry——!"

"I know," Damaris groaned. "I don't want him to want Blessing, but I can't marry him myself. I won't marry anybody; I *won't*! Ray, I couldn't give it all up! No one could expect that. Not now, when it's been given back to me! Ray, tell me what to do!"

"It's hard, Marry, dear. I do sympathise. But you'll have to choose."

"I have chosen. I'm going to dance."

"Then you can't try to keep Brian to yourself. He'd like a home of his own, and a family; he said so. You must be fair to him, Marry."

A sob shook Mary Damayris. "I didn't know— how much I cared—till you said that about Benedicta."

So she was awake at last. Was it advance or disaster? Surely it was better that she should understand?

"Then you do care, Marry dear!"

"Yes, I do!" Damaris sobbed defiantly. "But not enough to give up dancing. It's my whole life. No one has any right to make me give it up."

"He hasn't asked you to do that yet. But I think you'd need to give it up. He wouldn't want you to marry him, if you cared more for dancing than for him."

"I wouldn't want to do it. It wouldn't be worth while."

"No. He must come first, if you marry him."

"Well, he doesn't. Dancing comes first."

"Then you'd better not see any more of him. It's the only way. Was he taking you to Oxford, to-morrow?"

"Yes, but I shan't go. I'll ring up and say I'm not well."

"I shouldn't do that. Isn't it your last time?"

"Yes. It doesn't matter. I won't go."

"They'll want you for a final visit before we go north. That's going to be difficult, Marry. Brian's expecting to take us in his car and show us his house and garden."

"We'll go by train. I don't want him. He'll begin saying things, if he really feels like that about me."

"I don't know what he feels," Rachel cried. "He wouldn't look when you were dancing, I tell you, he looked at Benedicta all the time."

"Oh, that's rot!" Damaris said impatiently. "He may have looked at her, but he comes here to see me."

"We're talking in a circle and not getting anywhere. I'm going to warm some milk, and then we'll go to sleep and leave everything till the morning," Rachel said decisively. "Get into bed, Marry. There's no need to spoil your frock by lying on it."

She shook her head at the sleepy cats, as she waited for the milk to heat. "All very difficult. Poor Marry! She doesn't love him enough yet. But I believe she will."

She found Damaris in bed, so set the tray on her knees, and they shared the milk and biscuits in silence.

"Don't talk, Ray. There's nothing to say," Damaris said.

"Try to sleep, dear. Things may be clearer in the morning."

"I'm not going to Oxford in his car."

"No," Rachel said quietly. "I don't think you should. Perhaps we can put him off somehow."

She slept very little, and saw that the same was true of Damaris, when they met at breakfast.

"I shall ring up and say I can't go to Oxford," Damaris said briefly. "I'll make another appointment. They're going back to town this afternoon."

"They? Oh, yes, the Grandisons! You'd be better at Oxford," Rachel remarked. "Brian may come here during the morning."

"Then you must send him away!" Damaris retorted. "What you said last night was sensible. I don't want to see him. It's the only way."

"The only way to hide from him?" Rachel said to herself, as Damaris went towards the telephone. "Or the only way to find out how much she cares? If she means that, she's right. I don't think she can hide from Brian for long."

The phone rang and Damaris drew back. "Come and answer this thing. I'll attend to Oxford presently. I'm going to see if that rain in the night has done good work in the garden."

"Don't go too far. The call might be for you," Rachel warned her. "No, it's for me."

Damaris disappeared, and Rachel listened to Jen's voice. "Rachel speaking, Lady Jen."

"Ray, there's something I want Henderson to do in Oxford, and Ken doesn't need the car to-day.

So he'll take Dammy-Marry to her doctor. Will
that be all right?"

"Only too right, Mrs. Brown. Thank you, from
us both."

"Is anything wrong between those two,
Ray?"

"I had an attack of nerves last night and said
something that upset Damaris. I don't mean
that she's annoyed, but——" and she paused.

"You don't want to talk about her," Jen said,
with instant sympathy. "I only asked because
Brian's coming to see you, once he knows Mary
Damayris is safely off to Oxford. He asked me to
send Henderson and said he couldn't take her, as
he'd promised. It doesn't mean anything, I hope?
About you, I mean? We don't want to lose you,
and we don't want to break Dammy-Marry's
heart——"

"Don't worry, Mrs. Brown!" Rachel's tone was
firm. "Things are in a mess, but not such a mess
as that. If Brian's coming to see me, it's to talk
about Damaris. And I shan't leave the Abbey,
now or ever, unless I'm turned out."

"What a relief! But are you sure, Ray? About
him and Damaris?"

"I shall be, when I've talked to him. Damaris
isn't ready to give up dancing for him, but she
doesn't want him to marry anyone else."

"I see. But she can't go on like that."

"Of course not. But neither can she go all the
way yet, Mrs. Brown. She couldn't you know;
the idea is too new, and dancing has been her

whole life, as she says. Brian has to get over that hurdle. He must do it in his own way."

"I see," Jen said again. "It is hard for her. We'll wish them happiness and wisdom."

"I'm so glad you didn't say 'good luck,' Lady Jen."

"It's more than luck that's needed," Jen agreed. "Don't worry her; let her take her time. None of us will say anything. Tell her to be ready for Henderson at nine-thirty, as usual. Brian shall come to you at eleven."

"I'll give Benedicta her coffee at half-past ten and send her out to the garden before he comes."

"Good! How pretty she looked in that white frock last night!"

"I thought so," Rachel assented. "Thank you, from us all, Mrs. Brown."

She went to find Damaris and gave the message.

"Oh, well, I'll go, in that case!" Damaris sounded relieved. "I'll be glad to have it done. They'd have insisted on another appointment. I don't mind going with Henderson; he doesn't talk."

Brian arrived about eleven and met Rachel on the garth.

"No tourists, Sister Rachel?" He looked down at her. "You know that's what I want you to be, don't you?"

Rachel's face lit up. "I like my new name! I hope it will be mine in time, but you've a long way to go, Brian."

"I was afraid of that." He followed her into

the little parlour. "But I may hope for it some day, you think?"

Rachel looked at him frankly. "Damaris isn't ready yet. She cares for you, I am sure, but she still cares more for her dancing. You'll need to wait."

"I feared that, too," he said, gloomily.

"Brian, be sensible!" Rachel urged. "Dancing has been her only idea since she was sixteen; for six years. As she says, it has been her whole life. It was taken from her, suddenly and violently, and she very nearly broke her heart. Now it has been given back. Could you expect her to love any man so much that she would give up her career, just when it is opening again?"

"Why should she?" he broke out. "I ask myself that all the time. Why should she give up so much? Why should she care at all? She has everything; a great name, and work that she loves. Why should she leave it all, for me or any man? And yet—I want her, Rachel."

"She wants you too," Rachel said quietly, to comfort him. "But not yet enough to put you before her dancing."

"She could go on dancing. I'd be proud," he pleaded.

"I don't think she could, for long. It isn't merely the public shows. A dancer has to spend almost her whole life in practice. You'd have a very poor sort of wife! But even if you were willing, that's not the point. She won't marry

you as long as dancing comes first in her heart.
And you wouldn't ask her to do it."

"No," he admitted. "I'm not prepared to be a
poor second."

"You wouldn't be worth much, if you were.
I know you might be frightfully noble and say
you wouldn't interfere with her career, but you
wouldn't mean it. You'd always grudge her to
the public. Neither of you would be happy."

"It's all true, Rachel. Then I must wait. Is
there nothing I can do?"

"It's a very new idea to her. Give her time to
get used to it."

"But she must have known!"

Rachel thought of Marry's passionate cry:
"He comes to see *me*!"

"Perhaps she did know, but she hadn't faced
the thought. She's facing it now. Something
brought it home to her last night. Brian, tell
me! Why did you look the other way when she
danced?"

"Then she saw. Because it's the thing that is
coming between us; the thing that will keep her
from me," he cried. "It was more than I could
bear."

"I see. I wondered what was the matter."

"I'd never seen her dressed like that before,"
he said, struggling to explain himself. "The low
dress—she was beautiful. I'd seen her only in
working clothes or a morning frock, or in her
coat. I couldn't take my eyes off her. But when
she danced I knew what it was going to mean.

I could see what it meant to her. I couldn't watch her. I wish Mother hadn't asked her."

"It was hard for you. Brian, would you take us to Grasmere, as we'd planned, and then—it seems terribly mean to ask you——"

"Go on, please!" he said grimly. "You want me to come away and leave you there for your holiday?"

"Just that." Rachel looked at him apologetically. "I'm hoping that Damaris will miss you. She may find she cares more than she thinks. If you stay with us and try to go on as you've done here, being good friends and playing about, she'll be only too pleased, and you'll come home no further on than you are now. That's what she wants. She doesn't want to go on. But you do want it."

"I want her to have everything she wants."

"You don't, you know," Rachel told him. "You want a great deal more than she wants, at present."

He looked at her. "Sister Rachel, you're right. I'll do as you ask. It's a bitter disappointment! I've been looking forward to showing her my house and the garden, and to picnics with her and you on the fells. To come straight home and leave her will be a real blow. But I'll do it, if you advise it."

"We ought not to let you drive us there. We could go by train."

"Nonsense! Tell her I've unfortunately found some business that must be done, and I'll only be able to spare time to take you north. She must have her holiday in peace."

"But you'll leave your phone number with me, just in case——" Rachel began.

"If you feel that I could add to her enjoyment in any way, I'll come at a moment's notice, and I'll promise faithfully not to say anything that would distress her."

"You are more than kind! I'll be glad to be Sister Rachel to you," Rachel said earnestly.

CHAPTER XIX

DAMARIS SURRENDERS

LATE ONE EVENING Brian rang up the Abbey.

"Brian here, at the Manor. Is it all right about to-morrow? You're sure the early start won't upset you? I'll be round at seven."

"Six, if you like," Rachel assured him. "We'd much rather get up in the dark than arrive in the dark, and we don't want to spend a night on the way. But are you sure it's all right for you?"

"I'd like the early start. I don't want a night on the road."

"Then we think alike. It's more than kind of you. Can Lady Jen give you breakfast so early, or shall we stop somewhere for a meal?"

"We'll stop for several meals, but not for breakfast. Lady Jen and Kenneth say I can have it at five, if I like. They're preparing to take the family to the moors, and they're busy every minute. I'm going to see them at the Grange and meet the future Kenya settlers; that's what Kenneth calls their big boys."

"Then say half-past six here, Brian. We'll be ready."

"Good! Is Blessing going to take over the garden?"

"Of course. She'll do it well. When we come home she'll go to stay with her brother for a fortnight, and Damaris will carry on here. Madame won't be ready for her till mid-September. I say, Brian! Don't take any notice, if she's silent on the journey. She's feeling guilty about you; she says I oughtn't to let you take us, if you aren't going to stay and get some fun out of it. I don't think she believes in your important business."

"I don't, myself," Brian agreed.

"That's what Marry suspects. She says she'll sit behind with the luggage and I can chatter brightly to you in the front seat. I didn't make that up; it's what she said."

"You shall sit beside me," he agreed, "but I hope you'll cut out the bright chatter. I shall have plenty to do watching the road. I'm going at a good pace; we've a long day before us."

"I won't talk," Rachel promised. "We may not say much, but we're both deeply grateful to you."

As the car raced through the village next morning, an attic window was flung wide, and Benedicta leaned out, calling farewells. The girls waved to her; then they swept round the green and away on the road to the north.

"Now the garden's all mine!" Benedicta exulted. "And the Abbey, too. That old Miss Jenkinson hardly counts. She'll see to the tourists, but she hasn't a scrap of feeling for the Abbey. I shan't be lonely! I shall have Ambrose and Jehane and the other stories all to myself."

A week later Rachel sat alone on the rocky bluff looking down on Rydal Water. Damaris, in her shorts and pullover, and bareheaded, was tramping restlessly up the pass towards Hikers' Halt, where once they had lived and worked for a short time.

The holiday, so far, had been on those lines. Damaris had gone off alone, to tire herself out on the fells. Rachel, understanding too completely to feel hurt, had gone in another direction and had not teased her with questions when she came back.

But the trip was not being a success. Their beloved fells were as beautiful as ever, as green and brown and craggy; in places purple with heather. The lakes had their old dancing sparkle in sunshine, or were serene and peaceful at night. The climbing and tramping were still satisfying; and in the back of Rachel's mind was a warm, happy picture of home—the Abbey, the garden, the grey-walled parlour, with its colours and cosy comfort. She knew now that much as she loved the fell country, she wanted it only at intervals, for times of refreshment such as this was meant to be; if she was really to enjoy it, there must be home and work to which she looked forward when the holiday was over.

For herself all was well and she was entirely content. She looked down on peaceful Rydal and admitted it; she had found her place in the world and her job, and she had no wish to change. More stories were stirring in her mind, romances of this homeland; she would write them in the Abbey and would relive the days on the fells.

But she was far from content about Damaris. The holiday, for Marry, was a failure; she was restless and unhappy, unable to be still, trying always to work off the strong feeling that was surging in her. She spoke little, and was completely unlike herself. Rachel sympathised and understood, but could not help, except by silent forbearance. Talking would only do harm; Damaris must see this through for herself. If she loved Brian, as Rachel believed, how could she be happy while she was keeping him away?

They were lodging at Greylands, the farm next to their old house, Crossrigs. Rachel's first request had been for news of her black cat, Nigger, and she had sighed and smiled on hearing how he had died peacefully of old age.

"Just went to sleep, laying in your old garden under that there tree," Mrs. Green said. "He never had no pain or trouble; he was a-purring up to the very last. Quite content he was. I'll show you where we put him. I planted two bits of lavender for him and they're a-growing fine. Over twelve years you'd had him."

"I'm glad you didn't need to have him put to sleep. I'm sure you made him happy," Rachel said. "I've two young ones waiting for me in the south. I knew old Nigger had gone, but I've often wondered how he went. I'm thankful it was like that. How nice of him to go back to his own old garden! He always loved that little tree.

It was his very special place, and he remembered."

She rose at last from the rock by Rydal and took the paths that led back to Crossrigs. The high road, with its coaches and buses, was avoided by both girls whenever possible, and they knew all the tracks across the fells.

She was nearing the farm when a hail rang out from above, and Damaris came racing down the slope, a wild-looking object with curls flying in the wind. "Ray! I want you! Don't go in yet!"

Rachel stared at her. "Marry, what's the matter? Oh, Marry, what has happened? You shouldn't dash about among the rocks like that! You might fall and break something."

"Pouff! When did you or I ever fall on the fells? We're both like goats, as you know very well. Ray, I want you to send for Brian."

They stood and gazed at one another by the Crossrigs fence. Then Rachel took her sister's arm and pulled her into the deserted garden, close to old Nigger's little tree.

"Marry, what do you mean? What's happened to you? You're different, somehow."

"Can you get hold of him? Where is he?"

"At the Grange, with Sir Ken and Lady Jen. He was to join them to-day. But, Marry——"

"I want him. Do you think he'll come?"

"I know he'll come, as quickly as he can. Tell me, Marry! Something has changed you."

"I've changed my mind, that's all. Even if I have to do without any more dancing"—she caught her breath—"even then, I can't do without Brian."

She stared at Rachel, her eyes bewildered but radiant. "I don't know how it happened. I didn't think I could ever say that. But suddenly I knew, and it's true. He comes first. I can't do without him. Oh, Ray, I want him!"

Rachel caught her in her arms. "Marry, my dear! I'll ring him up at once. You shall have him to-morrow."

"Do you think I'm mad?" Damaris whispered.

"I thought you were, while you hesitated. You're wiser than you've ever been in your life before."

"Do you mean that, Ray?"

"I do! You're going for the biggest happiness —the one that will last. You could never be satisfied with dancing; not now."

"If Brian hadn't come——"

"You'd have been satisfied for a time. But however happy and thrilled you had been on the stage, you wouldn't be as happy as you will be now."

"It's something new," Damaris whispered. "I didn't know."

"Of course not. But you couldn't turn away from it now that you understand."

"I thought I could. But this week has been horrible!"

"And you just felt you couldn't bear it any longer?"

"Yes," Damaris assented. "I want him; that's

all. I don't know what's going to happen. I can't let Madame down altogether. But I've got to ask Brian what I must do."

"Madame will forgive you. She was very understanding when Daphne married."

"I feel an awful ass," Damaris said gloomily. "D'you remember how I went on about Daphne? I raved at her, didn't I?"

"You certainly scolded her! But Daphne knew and you didn't, at that time."

"You want Brian to come, don't you, Ray?"

"More than anything in the world," Rachel assured her. "I'm going to phone him, right now. We may have a decent holiday, after all. This week has been dreadful! Don't you want to speak to him yourself?"

"I couldn't! Oh, Ray, please! I should make an idiot of myself. It will be bad enough when he comes. I shall dash away and hide on the fells."

"Not you! Go in and dress yourself, while I run to the post office. No, I won't take you. I can't have you staring at me while I talk to him. I'll tell you what he says." And she raced down the road to the village, a song of joy in her heart.

Damaris watched her go, then went indoors to put on a frock. "I've done it now!" she murmured. "This is the end of Mary Damayris. But perhaps not just at once. I'll never be quite satisfied unless I go back and prove that I can do it. I'd always feel a failure. Ray won't approve, but I'll make her see it."

Rachel was back in half an hour. "He wanted

to come to-night, but he'd just arrived from London, so I wouldn't hear of it. I said if he came I wouldn't let him see you till to-morrow."

"As if you could stop him! Or me!" Damaris scoffed.

"Come in for tea. You must be looked after; you wouldn't trouble about it for yourself. Will you go off and leave me again this evening, Marry?" Rachel asked wistfully. "I've been so lonely."

"I've been a selfish pig," Damaris said remorsefully. "No, Ray, I won't. Let's have a boat and go on the lake."

"To-morrow night you'll go with Brian. But I shan't mind. You can give me to-night. To-morrow you'll belong to him."

"You are a lamb!" Damaris turned to her impulsively. "You've been lovely to me all along. Do you remember when we were here, years ago, before I'd danced in public? I knew what was coming to me—all the excitement and the publicity and, I hoped, success; and I said I should cling to you to keep me straight?"

"You said you felt like a birch tree in the wind and I must be your rock to which you'd cling," Rachel assented. "I've never forgotten, Marry."

"You've been just that. I've held on to you, and I'm doing it still, exactly like the birches on the rocks by Rydal."

"I was looking at them this afternoon," Rachel said.

CHAPTER XX

PICNIC FOR RACHEL

THE WATER of Grasmere was like a sheet of dark glass as Damaris rowed gently along by the bank. Rachel in the stern was content to be quiet, now that all was well.

"You won't mind, when I go and leave you?" Damaris asked suddenly. "We've been together all along. It seems frightfully mean to leave you alone."

"I didn't like your leaving me to be a dancer in London. I felt I ought to stand by you. But I want you to go, if it's with Brian."

"Did you use the key of the oratory that night?"

"Yes, but I didn't cry. I just sat and thought about you and felt lonely. Then I found Mary-Dorothy in the parlour, and we talked and I felt better."

"If I marry Brian——" Damaris began.

"Why if, Marry?"

"He hasn't asked me," Damaris retorted. "I may think he's going to do it, but it hasn't happened yet. Give us a chance!"

"Oh, well, all right! What were you going to say?"

"I suppose we'll live in his house at Ambleside. Will you live with us? Or will you stick to the Abbey?"

"How can you ask? Of course, I shall stay in the Abbey."

"But you'll come to us often. You'd better train Blessing as an Abbey guide; then she could take your place."

"Not a bad idea. She loves it already; she'd do the job well. Let's go to bed early, Marry. We've had an exciting day, and there's a still more thrilling one before you."

Damaris grinned at her. "Maybe! I wish you'd find somebody, too, Ray."

"It's not in the least likely," Rachel said calmly. "I'm not that sort. And I have too many men to want a real live one."

"In stories, do you mean? It isn't the same."

"No, but it's a very good substitute," Rachel retorted. "I'm always having new romances on my hands."

"You ought to have the real thing. Don't put me and Brian into a story!"

"No, I promise. Take us in now, Marry!"

"But I like this. It's so quiet and peaceful." She peered over the side into the dark water. "To-night's a sort of interlude between two bits of my life. Don't make me hurry over it!"

Rachel said no more, and they paddled gently up and down for an hour, hardly saying a word.

Then Damaris sighed, a sigh of pure happiness, and rowed to the shore. "I've been miserable all week," she confessed. "It's a great relief to feel better!"

"You'll feel better still to-morrow night,"

Rachel promised, as they stepped ashore, carrying the oars.

Damaris came down next morning to find Rachel busily cutting sandwiches, while Mrs. Green stirred the porridge.

"What are you doing, Ray? We can't go for a picnic! We must wait——" she paused.

"You must wait for Brian," Rachel agreed. "It's a glorious day. I'm going to walk to Ullswater."

"But——" Damaris stared at her wildly. "But you can't do that! And leave me?"

"You don't need me to introduce you to Brian! I know when I'm not wanted. You'll wait for him here. I'm going to Glenridding and Patterdale. If I'm tired I'll come home by bus."

"You mustn't! I want you! Oh, Ray, *please*!"

"Rubbish!" Rachel said briskly. "You'll fling yourself into Brian's arms and I should have to vanish. I may as well go at once and not waste the morning. He can't be here much before twelve, unless he gets up at dawn."

"Ray, stay with me!" Damaris pleaded. "I shall have an awful time, waiting alone!"

"I suppose you will. All the same, I'm going. If you take my advice you'll stroll along to meet him. Then Mrs. Green won't see your rapturous greetings. But keep to the road or you'll miss him. He might just possibly start very early."

"Ray, you're mean! You're horrible!" Damaris cried desperately.

"Not at all. This is your day and you must see it through for yourself."

"You can't go by that lonely track all alone!"

"What do you expect to happen to me?" Rachel jeered. "I'm quite as sure-footed on the fells as you are. You said we were both like goats. And the track won't be lonely—not in August. It's much more likely to be as crowded as the Strand. I shall get some tea with my lunch in Patterdale. You can think about Brian all morning."

No pleading could move her, and she set off half an hour later, swinging her stick gaily, a satchel slung over her shoulder.

Damaris, silent and apprehensive, went with her for the first mile. Then she turned back, as the path began to climb the steep green slope, and sat on the gate at the farm, watching Rachel's blue figure as she went slowly but steadily up the track, reached the rocky shelf, and picked her way carefully over the slate and loose stones.

At the gap in the wall, high up between Fairfield and Seat Sandal, Rachel turned, her hair blowing in the wind, to look over the wide view of mountains and lakes to the distant glimpse of sea. She waved her stick joyfully, and Damaris, far below, waved a white scarf in reply.

Then Rachel disappeared, on her way to Grisedale Tarn and eventually to Ullswater.

Damaris, with a breathless laugh, turned to go along the road. "Ray's all right now; going down is easy. The only bad bit is that rock slope and she's safely across. Now for it!"

Rachel sat by the tarn and remembered the picture hanging in her home in the Abbey. She tried not to think of Damaris and Brian, but found her mind returning to them constantly.

"Poor Marry! She really will have a bad time till he comes. But I couldn't help; it was better to come away. I'll get along; it's five miles down to Patterdale. With luck I'll be able to walk back. I'd like to do both ways."

Damaris met Brian quite an hour earlier than she expected. He had started at daybreak, sped on his way by the sympathy and good wishes of Kenneth and Jen.

She was sitting in the heather when the car came round the corner from Ambleside.

"Gosh—already! Can I stop him? He'll go on to Grasmere!" With no time to think she hurled herself into the road, waving wildly.

Brian drew up with screaming brakes. "That was risky, Pirouette. I nearly ran you down."

"I hardly thought you'd kill me. What time did you get up this morning?"

He grinned and opened the car door. "Hop in! I'm starving. Take me somewhere for a meal. Where's Sister Rachel?"

"Gone to Ullswater, across the fells."

He raised his brows. "It sounds like an adventure. Will she be all right alone?"

"Yes, rather! She wouldn't wait."

"That was like her. Where are you going to take me?"

"Langdale. Turn round and go back to Ambleside."

"Ambleside's too crowded. I want you to myself."

"Don't worry! Langdale won't be crowded. Martin Bernard will be after you with a stick, if you call me Pirouette."

"He doesn't mind. I'm a pal of Bernard's; nice chap! Tell me where to go. I don't know these parts yet."

They were soon running up the Langdale valley, Brian's eyes resting in delight on the lumpy Pikes before them. "I saw those first in your Abbey room."

"I've always been fascinated by them. But we came here by bus, or we walked. There's a good hotel."

"Ah, now you're talking!" Brian said. "And some lonely spot where I can tell you things?"

"Several." Damaris gave a low laugh. "I have things to say, too."

After lunch they climbed the stony track and sat by little Blea Tarn, and Brian told her several things. Then Damaris talked very earnestly, and he listened and agreed, somewhat ruefully.

"I believe you're right, Pirouette. But it means waiting, and I don't want to wait."

"Come home and tell Rachel! And to-morrow we want to see your house."

"Our house!" said Brian.

"Sometime; but not yet!" Damaris said firmly.

CHAPTER XXI

A RING FOR DAMARIS

"Then you did walk both ways! Aren't you dead?" Damaris greeted Rachel with a shout. She and Brian had waited at the farm till they saw her far above them, lest after all she should come by bus; then, recognising her, they had gone to meet her.

"Only a little weary," she said cheerfully, and held out her hand to Brian. "I'm so glad to see you! What have you two been doing?"

He gripped her hand. "Lunch in Langdale; I was starving. A long talk by a little lake——"

"Tarn." Rachel corrected him. "Small lakes are tarns. Was it Blea Tarn, Marry?"

"Sure. Now we're going to take you for a huge tea in Grasmere, a much bigger tea than Mrs. Green would give us! And then we're going to have a boat again; I told Brian about last night."

"You won't want me in that boat!"

"Sister Rachel, don't be silly," Brian said severely. "If I could marry you as well as the little Pirouette I'd do it, with young Blessing thrown in; I love all three of you. As that isn't allowed I'll have to be satisfied with one. But we aren't going to leave you out, especially to-night. We've all sorts of plans to tell you."

"For your house and the new rock garden?"

"I'm afraid not; not for some time." Brian's voice was suddenly grave.

Rachel shot a look at him. "I'll fall in with your programme, for this once. But I'm not going about with you all the time. I must go in and wash; I feel messy after my tramp."

Brian took the oars when they went to the boat and rowed to a quiet corner of the lake. "Now. Pirouette, out with it!"

Damaris leaned towards Rachel and spoke earnestly. "Ray, I'm going to marry Brian, of course, but not yet. I can't possibly let Madame down as badly as that! And I can't turn my back on ballet till I've proved to everybody that I can dance again. You do see that, don't you?"

"I don't see it at all! Do you mean that you want to go on dancing, as if nothing had happened?" Rachel cried.

"Just that; but only for a little while. I'm going back, to be Mary Damayris again and show the world that I'm all right and that I can dance as well as ever. Then I shall retire from the stage and marry Brian and settle down to make his garden."

Stunned, Rachel gazed at her and then at Brian. "What do you think about it?"

"I'd rather she didn't, of course. I want to be married to-morrow," he began.

Damaris shook her head at him. "Likely, isn't it? Mad, quite mad!"

"But I see how she feels," he went on. "And I want to be fair to her. If she won't be satisfied till she has made her reappearance on the stage, then I must wait."

"But will she give it up, if she goes back and has a big success?" Rachel asked doubtfully. "Won't it be terribly hard? You're risking a lot, if you allow it."

Damaris bristled at the word. "I don't belong to him yet!"

"I have to trust her," Brian said quietly. "If she finds she thinks more of her stage triumphs than of me I shall have to accept it. It would break my heart and spoil my life, but I can't tear her from her career against her will. She must be willing to come."

"Ray, be sensible!" Damaris leaned forward again and spoke urgently. "If I don't care more for him than for dancing I won't be worth much to him."

"As a wife," Rachel finished for her. "True, Marry. But you'll find it very hard."

"Then it's all the more worth doing! I'm not going to him feeling I've been a failure."

"You never were a failure; not for one second!"

"Well, then, feeling doubtful if I could still make good. I'm going back, and I'll make a success of it, and I'll make him proud. After all, he's never really seen me dance! When I go to him

I'll give him somebody of whom he can be proud, and I'll show him I care for him more than for the biggest kind of success. That will be worth doing!"

"If you do it, Marry."

"I shall do it. I want him more than dancing. If I could say that yesterday—and I did!—don't you think I can say it still more now? To-day has changed everything."

Rachel, looking at her, knew that it was true. Brian had taught her in his own way. She was triumphant and very sure of herself.

"It will be hard for both of you," Rachel said slowly.

"Look here, Ray! Do you think I'm going to have people say: ' Oh, yes! He married that poor girl who was hurt and could never dance again '! Not if I know it! They'll say: ' He married Mary Damayris, who made that marvellous come-back after her accident. She recovered completely and danced as well as ever.' And if they've any sense they'll say: ' She must have loved him quite a lot, to give up her career for him.' What about it, Brian?"

"It sounds better that way," he acknowledged.

"I'm not going through life as the poor girl who couldn't dance again, when I know I can! And I won't have people say I married you when I wasn't good for anything else!"

"Oh, Marry, they wouldn't think that!" Rachel cried.

"Yes, they would. They'd say: ' Oh, well, she's

found a husband, so it doesn't matter about her dancing!' They'd say I'd married him as second best. People would never believe I could have danced again; I'll have to do it to show them. And I will!"

"I don't want to be second in her mind to her dancing," Brian put in. "If she married me now, much as I should like it, I should always feel she might be regretting her stage career. If she makes good and then comes to me, I shall know she has put me first."

"Perhaps she's right. I hadn't thought of all that," Rachel admitted. "But I feel sorry for you both. You'll have a waiting time that will be very anxious and worrying, and she'll have a tussle with herself when she has to decide."

"It's up to him to make me feel quite sure I can't do without him," Damaris mocked. "He's begun well. At present I feel I can live without dancing better than without him. That's something for him to go on with! But I have to be certain of it, and I've had no dancing for two years. Until I've gone back and felt the thrill of it again, how can I be sure he really comes first?"

"It's that thrill I'm afraid of for you, Marry."

"It won't carry me off my feet this time! By then I shall be firmly anchored to Brian—or I ought to be!"

"You'll explain to Madame?" Rachel asked. "You must play the game. You can't let her put all that work into preparing you, and then give it up, unless you warn her what you're going to do."

"Ass! Of course, I shall tell her at once. Do you suppose I could dance with a guilty secret on my mind?"

"Guilty?" Brian asked, with a laugh. "Do you feel like that about me?"

"Only if I concealed you from Madame. I couldn't, anyway; she'd guess. You'd better find that ring you've promised me; it's to be emeralds, Ray. Then everybody will know."

"If you're going to wear his ring and be openly engaged, I shall feel happier," Rachel said.

"I expect he'll be about the theatre and studios a good deal. I'd better be engaged to him," Damaris said airily. "If I go back on him after that, everyone will know I chose dancing instead of him. Besides"—with a sudden change of tone —"I want everybody to know I'm engaged. I'm proud that he wants me."

"You should wait till you've got rid of me before saying that sort of thing," Rachel scolded. "Brian, if you'll put me ashore I'll walk home, and you can have her to yourself for an hour."

"You're not walking anywhere to-night, after tramping the fells all day, Sister Rachel," Brian said firmly. "We go together in the car. To-morrow will you come to see our house?"

Damaris chuckled. "'Our house' some day; not yet. We're both dying to see your house. It's called Heather Garth, Ray."

"I like the name. It reminds me of home," Rachel exclaimed.

"The Abbey garth. Yes, I thought of that," Damaris agreed.

CHAPTER XXII

BRIAN'S GARDEN

THE OLD grey house, Heather Garth, stood high
on a hillside, with a wide outlook over Windermere, a shining sea. A broad terrace lay in front,
and then the cliff fell away to the road, sloping
gradually at each side to give a carriage-drive up
to the door. Enclosed by the rock walls at road
level was a lawn, with a shallow pool in the
middle.

Both girls cried out in delight, for the rocks
were sprinkled with heather and gorse and golden
stone-crop, and the low wall between the lawn
and the road had harebells growing in the
crannies.

"The beginnings of a rock garden!" Rachel
said. "It could be made into a lovely place.
Everyone passing on the road would stop to look,
as they do at Maid's hill terraces."

"I feel it has possibilities," Brian agreed.

"More than that! It's waiting for *me*!" Damaris
proclaimed. "At the Abbey I had only a field to
work on, but this is made already, a natural rock
garden. Those cliffs could be covered with the
most gorgeously-coloured things, and there could
be banks of rock round the pool and sedums and
heaths all over them. It could look perfectly

heavenly! *How* I'll enjoy making it into what it ought to be!"

"It's yours, whenever you want to start," Brian reminded her.

Damaris shook her head. "Not yet; but some day. I'll look forward to it. Don't let it be spoiled, Brian! Take care of it! Is there any more up by the house? I smell—what do I smell?"

"I don't know what you smell, but I smell lavender," Rachel said. "Where is it, Brian? There's no lavender in sight."

"In the mixed garden behind the house. There's quite a lot——"

The girls were gone, racing up the sloping drive and round the side of the house. Brian laughed and followed them.

The vegetable beds and plots of perennials were edged with bushes of lavender in full flower. Rachel stood entranced, but Damaris, in wild enthusiasm, had grasped the possibilities.

"A lavender farm!" she shouted. "Oh, Brian! Root out those cabbages; you can easily buy them. Plant more lavender, masses of it, and grow it for the market! People will always buy lavender. You did mean to sell the rock plants and make a real business of it, didn't you?"

"It isn't necessary," he said. "But I felt it would be more fun to do the job in earnest and perhaps make the garden pay. Do you think the lavender would help?"

"Oh, much more fun! It would be a thrill to see which things people cared to buy. I'm sure the lavender would help. We'd sell bunches at the gate, and if we had more than we needed we'd supply the trade; the scent firms must use a lot. What a jolly place this could be!"

"Will be, some time," he amended. "But only if you come to help. I can't do it alone."

"Your experience at the Abbey will be useful, Marry," Rachel said.

"I've been preparing, without realising it," Damaris agreed.

"Come and see the house," Brian suggested.

"It's the garden I care about," the future mistress said frankly.

"You can't live in the garden," and Brian led them indoors.

Caretakers were in charge and the house was in good condition. Rachel exclaimed over the views of the lake and mountains, and Damaris admitted that it was a lovely house and could be made very comfortable. But at the moment her interest was out of doors and she was soon back in the garden, seeking out new treasures.

"I like the rooms and I love the broad window-seats," she told Brian. "But this thrills me more just now. Ray, look what's here!—a regular mat of lobelia, behind the lavender; isn't that luck? Just like at home!"

"We must tell the Lavender and Lobelia Queens," Rachel said.

As they sat together on a wide window-seat, looking out over the lake, Brian told of Jen's latest doings. "She drove down to Wycombe the day before she left home and carried off the little Manley girl, to spend a month on the moors and be company for Rosemary."

"Myonie? How kind of Lady Jen!" Rachel said.

"As if she hadn't enough with her own crew!" Damaris laughed.

"Apparently Lady Jen can never have too many, and Myonie's mother isn't very well. Some boys who were to have been at the Grange have gone to Mrs. Raymond instead, so there was room for Myonie."

"The Fraser boys. You don't know that part of the clan yet," Rachel agreed. "They're at school with Lady Jen's big boys, Andrew and Tony, but Mrs. Joan is their guardian, as their mother is in Ceylon. Myonie Rose will have a lovely time and it will do her a lot of good. I don't think Lady Jen can ever have too big a crowd!"

They returned to Heather Garth several times during the next three weeks, especially when rain came and picnics were impossible. Damaris roamed through the rooms and made plans, and Rachel gave advice which later proved valuable in turning the house into a home.

But for most of the time they were all three out together, and the holiday became a success, in spite of its bad beginning. Damaris, completely happy, stored up health and energy for a strenuous winter's work. Rachel watched her gladly, and gave in to her every wish.

In Brian's car they explored districts which had been out of reach to them before. Borrowdale and

the Langdales they had visited, but they returned
to them eagerly, and introduced Brian to Watend-
lath, with its tarn and waterfall, and to Tarn
Hows, up on the Coniston fells. There had never
been time or money to spare for long bus trips,
and Buttermere and Crummock Water had been
unattainable, though greatly desired. Brian took
the girls by Honister, to picnic near Buttermere,
and ran them out to Loweswater and home by
the Whinlatter Pass and Keswick. They led him
across the fells to Grisedale and Patterdale, and
later went by car through the Vale of St. John
and by Threlkeld and Troutbeck to Ullswater
again, and home by the other Troutbeck and
Ambleside.

They climbed Helvellyn and Catbells, to his
delight, and walked up the great Pass for tea at
Hikers' Halt with Miss Baldry; Brian had heard
the story of their adventure with her, and was
eager to see the cottage where they had lived.

It was a happy play-time for them all. Rachel
enjoyed the drives and picnic meals, but managed
continually to disappear and leave the other two
to amuse themselves in their own way.

"I had a lovely letter from Mrs. Grandison,"
Damaris said one day. "It was inside one to
Brian; she didn't know our address. She says she
knows it's a long time since we had a mother and
father, so she hopes I'll take her and Brian's dad
in their place and that they want me for their
own."

"Yes, we must remember you have a new family

now," Rachel said quietly. "I'm sure they'll welcome you and be good to you."

Damaris glanced at her. "It won't make any difference about you. You'll always come first."

"After Brian, I hope!"

"That's different. I like the Grandisons very much, but you and I belong; nothing will alter that. They want me to live with them, when I go to town next month, but I don't believe Madame will allow it."

"No, she'll want to keep her eye on you. But you could go to them for week-ends."

"I'm coming to you for week-ends! The Abbey is home," Damaris said quickly.

"I shall always want you. But Brian's people have claims on you, too. You must go to them sometimes."

"I'll think about it. I'd rather come to you. I say, Ray! Brian and I almost quarrelled last night! I said I should tell you," Damaris began, laughter in her eyes.

"Not seriously, evidently. What was wrong?"

"I told him that if we ever have what he calls 'a little Brownie '—a little girl of our own—we must call her Rachel Maidlin."

"Oh, Marry, dear! You didn't, really?"

"Of course I did. I know he wants to have her. I said you and Maid had meant more than anyone else to me. He said he was sure that was true and he liked the name, but he wanted the first to be called for me, and she must be Damaris Rose.

He's always wanted a girl called Rose, and we could ask Lady Kentisbury——"

"What a lovely name! I like Brian's choice better than yours. You must have Damaris Rose some day!"

"He said we could call her Dammyrose; we could even spell it Damirose. I said I'd like a Rose baby, to match all the others; and I told him that Lady Kentisbury had been a sort of god-mother to me. She gave me my dancing name; she was the first to call me Mary Damayris—do you remember? But I said Rachel Maidlin must come first; I couldn't possibly call our first for Lady Kentisbury and leave out you and Maid. He said you'd understand and Rachel Maidlin could come later. I said, no, I must have her first and we could wait for Dammyrose. Then suddenly we both saw how silly we were and we just shrieked with laughter."

"Idiots!" Rachel laughed too. "You've a long way to go before you have Dammyrose."

"Rachel Maidlin," Damaris said firmly. "Perhaps it will be worth giving up dancing for her sake."

"You'll certainly have to give up dancing, if you want her, whatever her name is," Rachel retorted.

CHAPTER XXIII

A BADGE FOR BENEDICTA

THE NEWS of Damaris's engagement was received with joy by the Abbey circle. Brian refused to drive all the way home in one day and insisted on a night at the Grange, near Sheffield, so Jen and Kenneth were able to give their congratulations in person.

Maidlin wrote joyfully to send her good wishes, begging them both to come to the Pallant as soon as they returned. "And bring Rachel, of course. Benedicta can carry on for one more day in the garden, and Miss Jenkinson in the Abbey."

Rosamund rang up the moment the news reached her, offering Vairy Castle in Scotland for the honeymoon. "But don't be married in February, for I couldn't be there, and I do want to see you married, Mary Damayris!"

"It won't be as early as February. I'm more likely to be making my come-back as *The Goose-girl* then," Damaris remarked. "Madame said six months' practice, but perhaps she'll relent and say I'm ready sooner than that. Bother our Countess's arrangements! I wanted to invite all the family. But it's something to have a place for our honeymoon, even if it isn't needed till next summer!"

"Spring," said Brian, when he heard the offer. "A castle in Scotland will suit me. We'll book it for May."

"We won't fix the date yet," Damaris told him. "I must play the game by Madame. I must give her a little time in return for all she's done and is going to do."

"I wake up in the night dreaming that you've had such a big success that you throw me over and decide to go on dancing for at least ten years."

"Well, you needn't, for it won't happen," Damaris said. "I'm keen to go back and show I can still dance, but I'm not going to stay; not now. I'm going to live with you at Heather Garth and grow lavender."

"And have Dammyrose?"

"If you go on like that, she'll be a little boy," Damaris retorted. "And anyway, she's going to be Rachel Maidlin."

"We shall have to toss up for it," said Brian gaily, greatly cheered by her tone.

Benedicta met them at the Abbey gate on their return. "Quite the big brother!" she mocked, as Brian helped the girls with suitcases.

"I hope so," he responded. "I've room for at least two little sisters, Blessing."

"Two? Oh, have you adopted Rachel?"

"Ray made me wild by saying perhaps he came here to see you, young Blessing," said Damaris.

"I don't want him! You're welcome to him. I can do with lots of brothers, but nothing nearer and dearer," Benedicta said cheerfully. "Come and inspect the garden! *My* garden, now!"

"Not yet. Mine for another fortnight, while you go to the seaside with your family," Damaris retorted. "And I can't let you off at once. We have to go to see Maid and Mrs. Joan and our Countess, and be kissed and congratulated. And I must go to see Madame and my new relations."

"O.K., Boss! I'll carry on for a few days more. I'm sure they all want to hug you," Benedicta agreed.

"Are my cats all right?" Rachel demanded.

Benedicta grinned. "Wait till you see! You've got three now. Mrs. Nigger has something to show you."

"Something as black as herself? I'm not surprised! Is she pleased?"

"Loves him. He's a little Nigger. The twins at the Hall have asked for him."

"Good! I don't mind having infants, so long as we can find homes for them. What does Rory say about him?"

"He's rather interested, but he pretends to despise both mother and son."

"I shall have to love him more than ever, while Mrs. Nigger is busy. He'll be lonely," Rachel said.

Rory met her at the door, golden plume erect, and gave her noisy and ecstatic greetings. He led her in to inspect the new arrival, and watched with solemn face while Rachel congratulated the

young mother and admired the blind baby, and
Mrs. Nigger sang in proud content.

Then Rory turned, rubbing on Rachel's legs, as
if he would say: "Come away from this nursery!
We're friends and we understand one another.
Babies are silly things, after all."

Rachel laughed and comforted him. "You and
I will be left alone, when Marry goes to town
and Mrs. Nigger is busy, old man. We'll be
company for one another."

"Yes, oh, yes! That's what I want!" Rory sang
happily, the rumbling roar in his throat louder
than ever.

When the family visits had been paid, Brian
took Damaris to town, for one day, and after
lunch with his parents they went to see Madame
Roskova.

"So, my child! You have changed your mind
and you will leave us," she scolded gently. "Oh,
là, là! But you look well and happy!"

"I'm both well and happy. Oh, Madame, don't
be cross! You did it yourself. Brian and I want
one another!"

"Well, we shall see. But you must wait, M.
Grandison. This girl must dance for us for a
time. She cannot come back for one night only."

"I realise that," Brian said ruefully. "But don't
keep her from me for too long, Madame."

"She will give us three months," Madame
decreed. "As she is leaving us, we will not train
her in any new role, but for three months we
will revive her own dances, *The Goose-girl* and

Rainbow Corner. No one has danced her parts; for two years those ballets have not been on our programmes. People will flock to see Damayris in her old place, and when they hear she has left the stage they will be glad to have had the chance to see her once more."

"Don't talk about him too much, Madame!" Damaris pleaded. "It's not a secret; look at my lovely ring! But I don't want to be ragged too fearfully."

"Teased you surely will be," Madame told her. "But you must bear it, my little one."

Rehearsal was in progress, so Damaris wandered in, with Brian, reluctant and amused, in her wake. She was greeted with shouts of joy, and all was noise and confusion at once. Her news had been passed round, for her letter to Madame had arrived a fortnight before, and reproaches were hurled at poor Brian by Bernard and others.

Irina Ivanovna, the Welsh girl whose real name was Irene Jones and who would dance with Damaris in *Rainbow Corner*, was full of scorn.

"First Daphne Dale and now you! Look you, Damayris, never did I think you would give in to a man!"

"Brian's rather extra special, Widow," Damaris said meekly, but with laughing eyes. "Thank you for your good wishes, though I haven't really noticed them! I'll be here to work in earnest in a fortnight. By then perhaps you'll decide to be kind to me."

"Nice people, all of them," she sighed, as Brian

took her home to the Abbey. "Brian, I could still make dances for Madame, couldn't I? We could run up to town for a few days, to stay with your mother, and your father could write the music; I'd tell him what I wanted, as I did for *Rainbow Corner*. I'd tell Madame about the dances and we'd start Elladella on them; Ella Delamere, that girl who looked so glum until she heard I wasn't going to stay with the company or have any new roles. Elladella has been one of their stars, since Daphne and I left, and she thought I'd come back to cut her out. Madame would train her in the new dances, and I'd come to town to crit. her in them. You wouldn't mind that, would you?"

"I haven't the right to object, Pirouette," Brian said. "It wouldn't be fair to drag you away altogether. Madame talked to me, while the crowd was buzzing round you; she says you have a great gift and it must be used. If you can use it by coming to town occasionally, without dancing yourself every night and spending your life in practising, then go ahead and good luck to you."

"You are a dear!" Damaris said fervently. "I may not want to do it. I may not feel driven to make dances. But I'm glad to know you won't expect me to stifle them, if they want to be made."

"You haven't felt the urge during these last two years?" he asked thoughtfully.

"Not once. I think I wasn't happy enough. But now that you've made me happy again, I think perhaps it will come back."

"How shall I know, when you are being driven to create?" he asked seriously. "Will you be terribly bad-tempered and irritable?"

Damaris gave a little laugh. "I'll tell you, if I feel it coming on. But it won't be at present; I shall be too busy with Madame. And for two weeks I have to take care of the garden while Blessing goes to the seaside."

While Benedicta was away on her holiday, helping Gail and Jimmy to entertain Penny Rose, her small niece, with sand castles and paddling, the school folk gathered at the Hall, in readiness for the autumn term. The twins, Elizabeth and Margaret, had been to North Wales with Jansy and Mary-Dorothy, to stay at the seaside house, Moranedd, near Plas Quellyn, and enjoy the company of Rob and Robin Quellyn and their small Bobbibach. They came racing through the Abbey to find Damaris as soon as they arrived.

"Mary Damayris, fancy going and getting married!" Jansy cried.

"But he's awfully jolly! We like him quite a lot," said Margaret-Twin.

"If you must get married, we're glad it's to Brian," Elizabeth added.

"I haven't done it yet. You're coming to see *The Goose-girl* again before I marry anybody," Damaris assured them.

When Benedicta returned, she spent one busy day with Damaris, making winter plans for the garden.

"I shall come home at week-ends to inspect your

work," Damaris announced. "But it's to be your garden now; I won't criticise. Here's my ' Abbey Gardener ' badge; sew it on the front of your working smock."

"I'm jolly proud of it." Benedicta took the badge joyfully. "And I'm going to be proud of my garden, too. Where am I to sleep? Does Rachel want me here for company, or do I stay with Mother Puddephat?"

They were having tea together in the Abbey parlour. Benedicta put her question innocently, but at once a quick look passed between Rachel and Damaris.

"Your job, Abbey Guardian. It's for you to say," Damaris remarked.

Rachel looked at Benedicta. "Blessing, if I wanted anybody, it would be you. And I don't mean to be unkind. But——" she paused.

"But you don't want anybody in Damson's place. That's all right! Don't worry about me," Benedicta said cheerfully. "I'd come, if you needed me. I love the Abbey I hope sometimes you'll go away to stay with Damaris and leave me in charge, and then I shall live here. But I know how you feel. It's your place and you want to have it to yourself. You don't want anyone instead of the Boss. Is that right?"

"Ray will be the Boss now," Damaris said.

"Not till you go away. Once you've gone I shall call Rachel Boss. Don't worry, Abbey Guardian. I've lived with my old lady for a year and I like her quite a lot. I don't mind going home at night. You aren't being unkind to me."

"You're sure?" Rachel asked anxiously. "Marry and I have talked about it. She doesn't approve; she wants you to come here, but I'd rather be alone. I shan't be lonely."

"And suppose you're ill in the night?" Damaris demanded.

"When am I ever ill in the night? I should ring up the Hall, and Mary-Dorothy would come flying to the rescue. But I'm never ill. In about forty years you may begin saying I can't be left alone at night," Rachel scoffed.

"Forty years!" Damaris looked at her in amusement. "Do you really think you'll still be taking people round the Abbey in forty years?"

"Why not? What else should I be doing?"

"Running your own home and looking after your family—but they'll be grown-up in forty years. Your grandchildren, then."

"Get out!" Rachel threatened her with the tea-pot. "Go back to your garden, before I pour this down your neck! I don't want grandchildren, thank you. You can have them. Is it all right, Blessing? You'll forgive me?"

"Sure! If I lived in the Abbey I should want to have it all to myself," Benedicta said. "I'll have the garden and you'll have the Abbey. Lady Joy won't be able to call it the Damaris garden any more."

"No, Benedicta's garden. I feel quite sad about it," Damaris assured them.

"You can think about the garden when you're

hanging on to the bar and waggling your legs in the studio," Rachel jeered. "I'd rather be Blessing and live in the garden."

"Oh, but you don't know!" Damaris retorted. "There are other things. *And* there will be Brian. But I shall think about the garden, and about his garden, too. I shall call yours the Garden of Blessing, Benedicta."

"Perhaps it will be, to some people, some day," Benedicta said hopefully.

CHAPTER XXIV

A SURPRISE FOR MYONIE

DAMARIS WAS GONE, in Brian's car, to begin her new life.

Rachel gathered up the remnants of the packing and set the house to rights. Then, determined to be cheerful, she went to her workroom and spread out her papers. A story written during their stay in the north had been corrected in the last fortnight and was ready to be typed, and she was planning a long letter to Marigold.

"Are you coming to help, Rory?" she asked the golden one, as he followed her. "Don't sit on my papers, please! Here's a cushion for you. You're missing Mrs. Nigger, I know, but she's busy just now. Wait a week or two and she'll play with you again. We both feel a little lost and forsaken, don't we?" and she stroked his soft shining head. "Never mind! Mrs. Nigger will soon have time for you, and Marry will come home for week-ends. Let's do some work!"

"Please, can we see the kitty?" asked a little voice at the door.

Rachel smiled at the two small girls, one in a blue cotton frock, the other in green. "Of course you can. When did you come home?"

"Last night, ever so late." Rosemary was

holding Hermione tightly by the arm. "Myonie's feeling rather gloomy, so I thought the kitty might cheer her up."

"And why is Myonie gloomy? Because you've had to leave the moors?" Rachel asked, putting her papers in a drawer. "Rory would sit on these, if I left them out. What's the matter, Myonie?"

" Want to go home," Myonie said, in a small voice.

"Her mummy isn't well, so she's going to stay with us," Rosemary explained. "She likes being with us, but she wants to see her mummy."

"I expect she'll go home soon. Come and see Mrs. and Master Nigger! They're very nice."

"And then will you tell us stories?" Rosemary begged. "That would be good for Myonie. Mother had to go out, so she told us to come and talk to you."

Rachel put away thoughts of her story for to-day. "I will, Rosemary. We're all feeling gloomy except you, for Damaris has gone and left me, and Mrs. Nigger won't play with Rory. So we'll cheer up one another."

"That will be nice," Hermione said gravely. "Brownie says you tell lovely stories."

"I hope nobody will come to see the Abbey. If they do, you'll have to scoot," Rachel warned them.

An hour later, Jen, leaving her car to go home without her, came from the Hall, where she had gone for a word with Joy. She crossed the garth from the tresaunt, and came quietly to the parlour door. Then she stopped, to gaze and listen and smile.

The small girls crouched on the rug beside the empty hearth, which was filled with a great jar of autumn leaves. Blue Rosemary, green Myonie, both gazed enthralled up at Rachel, who, in her white working gown, sat on a low chair, bending forward and talking earnestly. The three dark heads were close together; Mrs. Nigger and her baby in their basket were forgotten, but Rory was roaring happily in Rachel's lap.

"And what happened next?" Myonie whispered.

"Go *on*, Rachel!" Rosemary gave an excited wriggle.

"It's too bad to interrupt such a thrilling story——"

At the voice from the doorway all three started up.

"Oh, Mother! You've spoiled it!" Rosemary cried.

"It will keep," Jen said cheerfully. "But my news for Myonie won't. Myonie Rose, what do you think has happened? The loveliest thing! You have a baby brother, born this morning! I was the very first person to see him, after your mother and your granny. Isn't that grand news?"

Myonie stared at her and then jumped up with a shout and began to dance for joy. "A baby? Then there's two of us again! Oh, goody, goody! Is Mother pleased? When can I see him?"

"Perhaps to-morrow. Your mother wants to show him to you very much."

"That's splendid news for Myonie," Rachel said. "But what a surprise!"

Jen glanced at her and spoke quickly, while Hermione and Rosemary poured out questions so fast that they did not listen to what she was saying. "It's wonderful for Clover Manley. The father died six months ago and she had lost her first boy. When her husband went, after only two days' illness with pneumonia, she felt stunned and dazed, but she kept up long enough to come to live with her mother in Wycombe and to put Hermione to school. Then she was ready to collapse and felt as if she couldn't face what was before her or live without her husband. But Myonie came home from school and chattered about meeting Rosemary, and Clover began to think there might still be friendship left to her, if she could get in touch with those of us whom she had known at school. We asked her here, and then we heard all about it and I suppose we rallied round and took charge of her. I know we scolded her and told her to buck up for Hermione's sake and not go to pieces. Rosamund was particularly kind and asked her to Kentisbury and made a lot of her; Clover had always wanted to be a pal to Ros at school, but somehow it didn't happen. She was shy and merely admired Rosamund from a distance. It happened this summer and they are real friends now. Geoffrey and Ros are to be godparents to the new baby, so, as Rosamund says, she is officially godmother to Clover's boy and ' not 'fishly,' to quote Rosemary, to her girl."

"What's he to be called?" Hermione made herself heard.

"John Geoffrey Manley. John is for your daddy and Geoffrey is for his godfather."

"Uncle Geoffrey?" asked Rosemary. "Roddy's daddy?"

"Yes, Roddy's daddy. If you two come home at once, there will be time before the post goes for Myonie to write a tiny letter to her mother."

"Couldn't I write to John at the same time?"

"You certainly could, Brownie. But his mother will have to read it to him. She's so pleased to have a man in the family again!" And Jen smiled across at Rachel. "I hope John won't be completely spoilt!"

"Can we come back to-morrow for the rest of the story, after Myonie's been to see John?" Rosemary pleaded. "Or will she stay with him, now?"

"No, she'll come back to us for two or three weeks. Her mother will be busy with little John. Myonie can go to school with you and Mike. Will you tell them the rest of the story to-morrow, Rachel? Or are they taking up too much of your time?"

"They shall have the story," Rachel promised. "But Myonie must tell me about Baby John, too."

When Rosemary and Hermione arrived next day the twins from the Hall came too. "We want to hear that story," Elizabeth protested. "Why did you leave us out? Brownie told us about it;

D.F.A.   N

we know the first part. We want to hear the rest."

"You're too old for my stories. Great tall girls of thirteen!"

"We aren't too old; we aren't!" Margaret shouted indignantly, with a return of her baby vehemence.

"It was about girls at school. We're girls at school. We liked it," Elizabeth declared. "Go on with it, please, Rachel. What did they do next?"

"Aunty Jen says she heard a bit of it and it was a jolly good yarn and quite exciting," Margaret cried. "We're ready for the next chapter, Rachel!"

Rachel's story, continued from day to day, became famous among the younger children, and for the next week, until school began, Rosemary and Myonie, and the twins, spent hours in the Abbey, listening to the romance, which was partly invention and partly remembered from her own schooldays. Jansy had gone home to see her mother and small brothers and sisters and the Fraser boys, and when she returned to the Hall she declared that she would have liked to hear the story too, even though she was going to be fifteen at Christmas and was growing so tall.

"You! You're almost grown-up!" Rachel protested.

"Not when you're telling stories," Jansy retorted. "I know when I'm lucky! You must start another one, and we'll come and listen in the evenings, when it's dark."

One night before school began they stayed later than usual, and Mary-Dorothy came to fetch them home. She stood in the doorway, as Jen had done, and listened, raising her brows at what she heard. Then she collected the audience and carried them off to bed, handing Rosemary and Hermione over to Kenneth, who had come to take them through the park.

Then Mary went back to the Abbey. "I've come to talk to you, Rachel."

Rachel, preparing her evening meal, looked up joyfully.

"You've come to supper, I hope. I'm not lonely, but I do like to see you here, Mary-Dorothy."

"You're sure you aren't lonely? We're not quite happy about your being alone."

"I'm quite happy about it! I like it. I have Benedicta for meals, and she's there in the garden if I want her. Rory is a real companion and talks to me all the time, though Mrs. Nigger isn't much use at present. And I've seen so much of those jolly kiddies lately. I'm glad they've begun to come."

"That's what I want to say to you. Ray, why *don't* you write that story down?"

Rachel stared at her. "That school stuff? Not worth while. It's only to amuse our little crowd."

"They're completely entranced by it. I've heard bits from the twins and to-night I heard a little for myself——"

"You oughtn't to have listened," Rachel protested. "It's not meant for you!"

"It's as good as anything of mine. If you don't make it into a book I shall be deeply disappointed in you."

"I'd hate you to be disappointed," Rachel jeered. "But I can't believe it would be worth while."

"Sit down!" Mary commanded, and lifted the golden cat out of a chair to make room for herself.

He leapt into her lap and tramped up and down, and then curled round and sang himself to sleep, while Mary spoke earnestly. "Ray, my books are for girls, not for grown-ups, but I've felt it worth while to write them——"

"But yours are good! They're the real thing!"

"Yours would be the real thing, too. I've never dared to think I could help grown-ups; I doubt if I could even amuse or interest them. But it has seemed worth while to try to influence girls and children for good, by amusing them and catching their interest. Girls are the grown-ups of the future. They may keep something of what is put into them while they are fresh and receptive. I've believed it was more worth while to write for them than to try to write novels."

Rachel gazed at her, deeply interested. "I'm sure you're right, Mary-Dorothy. But it would never have occurred to me to make that school stuff into a book."

"You could do it," Mary insisted. "You'd have to take it seriously and put more work into it than you do when it's just to be told to our children. But I know you could do it. What has happened to that novel you were writing?"

Rachel flushed; Mary thought she winced. "I finished it and sent it out. Several people have seen it. They say they like it quite a lot, but not enough to publish it. I shall stick to shorts. There's more satisfaction in them."

"Only in some ways. You see them complete and you get them published. But they mean endless plots, and you can't have as much pleasure in the characters as you would in a book. You don't live with them long enough."

"A book would be more satisfying than anything in the world! But it doesn't seem to come my way."

"Do a book for girls," Mary advised. "I'll tell you where to send it. Feel the importance of girls; then it will seem worth while. Think it over, Ray! I'd like your stories to reach a wider public than our little crowd."

"It's a new idea, and a very odd one," and Rachel prepared supper with thoughtful eyes.

Mary knew she had said enough. "What news from Damaris?" she asked.

"Oh, very good! Madame is satisfied with her work and thinks she may be ready to dance by February. The Grandisons want her whenever she is free; she has been to them for the last two week-ends and says she feels quite one of the family. I'm completely happy about her. It's such a relief!"

"Happier than you were when she first went back to town?" Mary smiled.

"Heaps! Brian has made all the difference. She's so very happy with him."

"Won't she find it hard to give up dancing when the time comes?"

Rachel looked grave. "I'm afraid she will. I believe she'll do it, but she'll find it very difficult. She may try to put it off and have a few months longer on the stage."

"That would be hard on Brian."

"Yes," Rachel said soberly. "There's no date fixed, you see. She means to marry him, but— well, we'll hope for the best!"

CHAPTER XXV

SEARCH FOR A QUEEN

"You DID a good bit of work for several people when you set Rosemary to look after Hermione Manley." Rachel smiled at the tall May Queen, Rosalind Kane.

Queen Lavender had missed the first few days of the term. A double wedding had taken place at Kentisbury, and she had been bridesmaid to one of her dark twin sisters, Amanda Rose, while Roddy had been page to the other, Araminta Rose. Now Mandy and Charles Harvey had gone to Vairy Castle for a fortnight, and would then go on to Edinburgh to look up old friends; while Minty and Dick Grayson went cruising in his yacht for their first two weeks, and then would go to Vairy to finish their holiday.

"Vairy is really becoming what we hoped it would be," Rosamund had said. "I call it Honeymoon House. I suppose Damaris and Brian will be the next couple to go there!"

The greater part of Rosalind's holiday had been spent with her married eldest sister and her little niece, to whom she was godmother. Now she had come back to school to finish the second year of her cookery course and for her two winter terms as Queen. Her hair was coiled in big plaits over her ears, for she was eighteen and a half, and she looked grown-up and thoughtful, more than ever like Rosamund, her aunt.

As soon as she could spare time she came to Rachel's Abbey parlour to hear about Damaris and Brian.

"Rosemary and Hermione? Yes, it has turned out well," she said, in reply to Rachel's remark. "I was sorry to miss the first few days—that's when the Queen is really useful! But I had to see our twins married, and Jansy promised to look out for new girls. Now I find that Rosemary and Hermione have decided to play at being Queens and see that nobody is as lonely as they were when they were new. 'Of course, it won't be like me and Myonie,' Rosemary said. 'We're friends! But we'll take care of new girls and make them be friends with one another, like you did us.' It's nice of the babes."

"Future Queens?" Rachel smiled.

"In six or seven years, perhaps! Rosemary is much less reserved than she used to be. Isn't Myonie pleased about the baby? It's a lovely story!"

"A happy one, after all. And you helped it on by throwing them together."

"I expect it would have happened." Rosalind sat silent, staring at the little fire Rachel had kindled.

"Troubles at school?" Rachel asked presently.

"Not exactly, but I don't know what to do. I'd like to hear what you think."

"I'll feel it a real compliment, if you'll ask me."

Rosalind lifted Mrs. Nigger into her lap. "Where's the baby? Come along; I'll hold you both, and Uncle Rory can sit on Rachel. Now we're all happy!—It's about the next Queen, Rachel."

"Isn't it early to think of that? It's a long while till May."

"Yes, but if I knew who she would be I might be able to help her. Usually the abdicating Queen is still at school and can back up the new one, but I shall be leaving, and they won't have Jean or Marigold, and Jansy will be only fifteen. She and the new Queen will feel very much alone."

"And you'd like to train your successor?"

"I might prepare her a little. But I've no idea who will be chosen."

"No idea at all? Does nobody show signs of being suitable?"

"I can't see anyone. I'd like Tessa to be Queen, but——" and she paused.

"Tessa? Isn't she the senior whom you had to fight over the question of skirts or tunics, this time last year?"

"How wonderful of you to remember!" Rosalind exclaimed. "Yes, Tessa was the leader of the opposition, till we won her over. She's joined us as a Cookery student this term, so I see a good deal of her. She'd make a fine Queen in lots of ways, and the girls like her. But——"

"Why all these buts?" Rachel demanded. "What's the matter with Tessa?"

"She fools about," Rosalind said simply. "She won't take anything seriously. She's so glad to be done with ordinary school work that she just plays and makes an ass of herself. I've heard the girls say: 'Tessa would be all right, if she didn't act about so.' I've even heard—'Tessa would be quite a decent Queen next year, if she would only stop being a goat.' She's so silly; she won't be steady and sensible."

"You've really heard that said—that she could be a good Queen?"

"Oh, yes, the girls have said it. They often talk about the next Queen. They've asked me what I think, but I had to say I didn't know yet."

"What does Jansy think?"

"That the Club would like another senior better than anybody younger, and that Tessa's the right person, but that she isn't responsible enough. The girls wouldn't look up to her."

"There are still two terms. You'll have to speak to Tessa," Rachel said decisively.

"But what can I say? I can't ask her to steady up so that she can be Queen, for I don't know that she'll be chosen."

"Would she like to be Queen?"

"She'd give anything to be Queen." Rosalind spoke with conviction.

"Then you must tell her exactly what you've

heard; that some of the girls would choose her, if they felt she'd be a good one, but that at present they're doubtful and that it rests with her whether she's asked or not. Rub it in that it's only some of them and that there may be other candidates, for all you know. She'll understand that you can't say anything definite. But she ought to know and have the chance to pull herself together. She just hasn't thought."

"I don't like doing it. It seems like criticising her."

"You can't possibly let Tessa ruin her chances by not giving her warning," Rachel said. "You'd always regret it."

"I suppose I should." Rosalind sounded doubtful, however.

"Suppose you shirk it and say nothing, and when May comes there's no girl suitable and they have to put up with someone quite inadequate? I suppose that has happened in the past?"

"Once," Rosalind said briefly. "I've heard about it. There was one failure, a slack Queen. The girls are quite sure about that. Never mind who it was! She's left now."

"You'll leave school next May, but you'll come back for coronations with your aunt, and you'll hear about the Club from Jansy and others. Suppose the next Queen is another failure, how will you feel? You'll know Tessa could have been a good Queen, if she'd tried; and if she's so keen she will try, once she understands. You can't let the Club down like that, Lavender."

"You feel I shall be funking, if I let Tessa go on playing about?"

"I do. You have a real chance to help the Club. You'll take it, of course."

Rosalind sighed. "Being Queen isn't always easy. I like helping people and making them be friends, but I don't like finding fault."

"It won't feel like finding fault," Rachel assured her. "It's all in the way you do it. Tessa will probably fall on your neck in rapture and promise to be the meekest senior in the school."

Rosalind laughed, in spite of herself. "It will be a shock to everybody, if that happens. Yesterday she tried to put salt in her cakes instead of sugar; we just stopped her in time."

"How childish!" Rachel exclaimed. "You can't let her go on like that! Here's an idea for you, Nanta Rose!"

Rosalind smiled across at her. "My old baby name! Jansy still uses it. Tell me your idea, Abbey Guardian!"

"A very small one. Ask Tessa to tea on Saturday; here, not at the Hall. There are too many children at the Hall. I'll give you tea, and you can take her into the garden for your talk."

"I'd like that," Rosalind said gratefully. "Will you show her the Abbey?"

"Hasn't she been round? I'll take her, of course. You'll find it easier to talk here."

"It wouldn't be easy at school. It is good of you to help so much!"

"That's what I'm here for; partly, at least.

Don't be frightened about tackling Tessa! Her keenness to be Queen will help," Rachel said. "I may have to be with tourists; Saturday is our busiest day. But I'll have time to get your tea ready, and you can look after Tessa."

CHAPTER XXVI

CONSULTING THE ABBOT

As Rachel had foretold, she was kept busy on Saturday afternoon, but she seized a chance to make tea for the girls, and left Rosalind installed at the teapot, with Tessa, highly delighted, as her guest. Presently she saw them go out to the garden and walk up and down the narrow paths, talking earnestly. Benedicta had been warned to keep out of their way, so she worked steadily, cutting down phlox and golden-rod and carrying them to the rubbish heap, and left the schoolgirls alone.

Rachel dismissed a party at last and hoped no more would come. She was putting on the kettle again to make tea for Benedicta and herself, when Queen Lavender came to the doorway.

"May I help? We cleared away our dishes and washed up."

"I saw that, and I blessed you for it," Rachel responded. "Where's Tessa?"

"Gone home; she cycled here. It's going to be all right, Rachel. Thank you a thousand times!"

"Oh?" Rachel smiled at her. "Tessa wasn't upset?"

"She was pleased. It was as you said—she saw I was trying to help her to be Queen and she wants that just terribly much. She won't be an idiot any more."

"She knows she may not be chosen?"

"Oh, yes! She knows I couldn't promise anything. It's still so far off. But she sees how she was making the girls feel about her—as if she was the clown at the party, was how she put it. And she knows you don't ask the clown to be Queen."

"She'll be all right now. I'm so glad, Nanta Rose!"

"If the Club has her for Queen she'll be a good one. She has so much in her, but it has to go in the right direction."

"Yes, it was being wasted. You've done another good bit of work, for the Club this time."

"You did it, really. I've promised we won't say a word to anyone, even to Jansy. Tessa can't have people saying she's trying to be made Queen," Rosalind pleaded.

"Of course not. I won't say anything. All we've done is to stop Tessa spoiling her chances."

"She told me what colours she'd choose," Rosalind laughed. "Most girls know what kind of Queen they'd like to be, even if they're certain they'll never be chosen. I knew, and Jansy knew, but neither of us expected to be Queen."

"What would Tessa be?"

"The Lupin Queen, and the girls can call her ' Wolf,' if they like. Lupin means a wolf, doesn't it?"

"It does," Rachel agreed. "Another blue Queen?"

"No, we've had so much blue lately, with Forget-me-not and Lobelia and Rosemary-blue and my lavender. Tessa's train would be lemon-yellow; lovely with her short dark hair! But she'd have long spikes of lupins stretching from the corners, in blue and rose and apricot. She says she'd want something gaudy, or at least exciting, after my 'demure lavender'; that's what she called it; and after Jansy's dignified deep blue. Jean's rosemary colours were sober, too. Tessa thinks it's time the procession was brightened up."

"Her lupin train would certainly be striking," Rachel agreed. "I think it would be rather hand-some, and she'd look lovely. Lobelia—lavender—lupin! You'll have laburnum or love-in-a-mist next!"

"Or lettuce." Rosalind laughed. "Lily of the valley would be prettier."

"But you'll need to keep all that a secret, Nanta Rose."

"Oh, yes! Tessa must tell people herself. Here's a car; oh, Rachel, won't you get any tea?"

"Bother! It's almost six. How thoughtless people are!" Rachel lifted the kettle off the stove and turned to the door.

A hail greeted her. "Rachel—ahoy! We haven't come to see the Abbey! Don't panic!"

"Marry!" Rachel cried. "I didn't expect you to-day! And Brian! How lovely to see you!"

"Not so lovely. We've come for your advice, because we've had a terrific quarrel. Everyone comes to consult the Abbot, so why shouldn't we?"

Rosalind fled through the Abbey and disappeared. "I'm not wanted! I wonder if Mary Damayris means it? Another thing I must keep to myself!"

"Marry, what do you mean?" Rachel demanded. "Brian, what is she talking about? She isn't serious, surely?" at sight of his grave face.

"I shouldn't call it exactly a joke," he admitted.

"Come inside!" Rachel said firmly, and closed the parlour door on the world. "Have you had tea? Because I haven't. I was just going to call Benedicta."

"We're going to have tea with you," Damaris began. "But only you. We can't talk before Blessing."

Rachel pursed her lips. "Then you'll have to wait. Blessing is working hard and she must be fed."

She prepared a tray with food and dishes, made a small pot of tea, and carried it out to the garden. "Do you mind very much not coming indoors? Damaris and Brian seem to want to talk."

"O.K., Boss! It's lovely out here. I'll sit on Wirral and use a red stone for a table." And Benedicta arranged herself in comfort. "You've

D.F.A. O

even brought the book I'm reading! This is
luxury!"

"I think you have everything you'll want."
And Rachel went back to the parlour, looking
worried.

"Something wrong," Benedicta said to herself.
"What has Mary Damayris been up to? They
don't want me, that's certain!"

"Wait!" Rachel said briefly to Damaris. "Go
on waiting! I need my tea, and I expect you want
yours."

She would not let them talk for several minutes.
But at last she said gravely, "Now tell me what
this means! I thought you always wanted to see
the Saturday night show?"

"Yes, but we wanted to see you more."

There was a pause. Damaris did not seem to
know how to begin. At last she said defiantly,
"I've asked Brian to marry me at once—quietly,
of course—and he won't do it."

"Damaris!" Rachel cried, breathless with shock.
"Are you quite mad?"

"Not a scrap. He says he wants to marry me.
Why shouldn't he do it now, when I've asked
him?"

Rachel looked at Brian. "I'm glad you had the
sense to keep your head. What does she mean?"

"It isn't easy," Brian groaned. "I want her
more than anything in the world, but she won't
believe it."

"Then why don't you do as I ask?" Damaris
wailed. "Ray, I'm not mad. I'm afraid! Dancing

is getting hold of me again. I want to belong to him and feel safe."

Rachel stared at her. "I was afraid of that. Do you mean that you'd marry Brian now and give it all up? It would be hard on Madame and everybody."

"I couldn't, of course. I couldn't let them down. I must go on, as I've promised, but I want to belong to Brian, so that—so that——"

"So that she'll have to give up the stage in June and come to me, whether she wants to come or not," Brian said grimly, his jaw set. "I won't do it. I don't want an unwilling wife. Suppose we marry, and the pull of the stage becomes too strong, and she doesn't want to leave?"

"I should keep my word," Damaris cried. "I always play the game! If we were married I'd stick to my part of the bargain!"

"Yes, you'd do that," Rachel interposed, before Brian could speak again. "But you might try to put it off for a month, and then another month, and then till the end of the summer."

"Then he doesn't trust me!"

"I trust you absolutely. That isn't the trouble," Brian said. "You'd keep your word and you'd give up your work and come to me. But it might be because you had promised—as a duty—not because you wanted to come. I want you to love me more than ballet-dancing."

"I do! You know I do! But it gets me, some-how, and—and I thought if we were married

I'd feel safe," Damaris said breathlessly, very near to tears.

"I don't want to hold you, if you don't want to come to me."

"I do want to come! But I don't trust myself," Damaris half sobbed. "You don't know how hard it is!"

Rachel took her in her arms. "Cry, if you want to, Marry, dear. I won't scold any more. I told you it would be hard for both of you. But you mustn't quarrel with Brian. Don't even make jokes about having quarrelled with him! You love one another far too deeply for that."

"He doesn't believe it." Damaris shook, and hid her face.

"Oh, yes, he does! It's because he loves you so much that he won't do this to please you. He wants you altogether, the whole of you. If he took you now he'd never feel quite sure you had put him before dancing. Can't you see that? You want him to be sure. You love him enough to want to give him your very best, don't you?"

"Of course I do!" Damaris said indignantly.

Rachel shook her head at Brian, who was trying to speak.

"Your best is yourself, without any regrets for your career, and given freely, when you are at the height of that career. Not now, when you haven't tried. You may fail, when you dance again——"

Damaris quivered impatiently. "Don't be an idiot! I shan't fail. I know!"

"Then you'll have all the more to give to Brian. You'll have a big success and a triumphant short season, and then you'll go to him, because you know he can make you happier than the stage could do, and because you want to make him happy. Can't you see that if he married you now, you would feel he didn't trust you and so he had to make sure of you?"

"I want him to make sure of me!"

"Yes, but he doesn't. He would feel he hadn't trusted you enough; and you might come to feel it, too. Everybody would say it. 'He thought he'd better make sure of her,' Bernard and Antoine would say; perhaps Madame too. Brian couldn't bear that."

"I don't care what people would say."

"You have to care, sometimes. And it would be what Brian himself was feeling. You're being very hard on him, Marry."

Damaris lay silent in her arms. "I didn't mean that," she whispered at last.

"He wants to do it, you see. He wants to marry you and hold you that way. But when the time came for you to leave the stage, he'd always have the fear that if you hadn't been married you might not have been willing. That isn't lack of trust; how can he know? If you had been married at once, when you were first engaged, I'd have thought it quite wise, but I'm not sure that he would, although I know it's what he wanted. He'd have felt he was keeping you away from the temptation of the stage and that you might regret it. I think now you were probably right to insist on going back. It was your choice; he gave in to you. Now you must see it through, or else back out altogether. Surely your love for him is strong enough to last six months and to resist even the pull of the stage?"

"I'm not sure of myself," Damaris groaned. "I wanted him to help me."

"Rachel, I'll do it, if you think it would be wise," Brian said, at length.

"I don't think it would be wise. Damaris has grit enough to see this through without falling back on you. She's had an attack of nerves, that's all. You may as well know what you're going to marry! She's like that—up or down. She's been thrilled and happy about you and about starting dancing again; now she's suddenly gone all frightened because she loves it so much. She loves you more, but still, the dancing pulls her very hard. It was bound to happen. But you come first, and she won't give you up. Isn't it true, Marry?"

"Yes," Damaris whispered. "It's true, every word, and I'm an awful ass. I'm sorry, Brian. I'll forgive you for not marrying me when I asked you."

Brian's lips twitched. "Pirouette, if you could know how I long to do it!"

"I'll make you proud," and Damaris sat up and brushed the tears from her eyes. "I'll make you say: 'Am I really going to have that girl for my wife?' And I won't be your wife till I have made you say it. But when I've succeeded, and when I've played the game by Madame and Antoine, then I'll come, whenever you ask me."

Rachel kissed her. "You'll both trust one another, and you'll marry Brian when the time comes because you're ready to do it, and not because you're afraid ballet might take you away from him. And he'll know you want him more than anything in the world, for you'll have given up everything for him. Are you going to the Manor?" and she looked at Brian.

"I thought perhaps they'd put me up and I could run Pirouette back to town to-morrow."

"They'll be glad to see you. I'm going to talk to Blessing." Rachel went to the door.

"Don't tell her I was an ass!" Damaris cried.

"I won't tell anybody," Rachel promised, and went out and left them together.

"Anything wrong?" Benedicta asked.

"Not serious. They disagreed about something, and they wanted to consult me."

"Abbot!" said Benedicta. "I was the first to call you that."

"Abbess would be more suitable, Blessing."

"No, Abbot," Benedicta said firmly.

CHAPTER XXVII

A CROWN FOR TESSA

RACHEL WENT TO Brian, as he was starting up his car.

"Don't worry too much about this, Brian! You've come up against Mary Damayris; it had to happen. She has this temperamental side; she really is a very great artist. But it's called into life by ballet; when she settles down in the country she's quite a different person. Her first plan was to live on our old farm and keep hens and bees, and that side of her is normal and happy and jolly. It's the side you'll see most, when you live together and make the garden at Heather Garth. But she's very sensitive; you'll understand when you have really seen her dance."

He looked down at her. "I love all the sides of her, Sister Rachel. Was I wrong to refuse? You can't know how much I'd have liked to marry her on the spot!"

"I can guess." Rachel smiled at him. "It was very hard for you, but I'm sure you were right. You might both have regretted it."

"I shall be anxious for the next six months," Brian said grimly. "Ballet may conquer, after all."

"I don't believe it. She loves you too much. But I shall be anxious, too," Rachel admitted. "And it will be worse as time goes on and Damaris grows more enthralled by her dancing. All the same, I trust her, and you must do the same."

"You'll never tell anybody I was an ass, will you, Ray?" Damaris asked anxiously, as she went to Brian's car next day. "Things told to the Abbot shouldn't be repeated!"

"The confessional!" Rachel agreed. "I won't tell anyone, Marry dear. But don't be so silly again."

Damaris did, indeed, become more deeply involved as the months of training wore on. She felt her powers returning, and Madame and Antoine were enthusiastic over her progress. She would be their Goose-girl and teasing Fairy once more, but—said Madame—with something added, a depth of feeling born of those months of tragedy and despair and of her new happiness. She was radiantly happy, whether with Brian or without him; he had to admit that just now he was not necessary to her, so far as he could see.

Rachel thought otherwise, and tried to comfort him. "I believe Marry is so happy just because, behind all the work which she enjoys so much, she has you," she said. "She only had me before; she's conscious of something new. Her happiness is rooted in you now, and it has changed her. She is dancing better; Madame says so. She is more balanced; it gives her greater depth."

Brian hoped she was right, but he did not feel

sure. He was rigidly determined that Damaris should be free to make her choice and even to end her engagement, if she felt she could be happier without marriage, and he would show no jealousy of her work or make any criticism. When they were together, which was whenever Madame would spare her from practice, they talked of the old house to be made into a home and the garden to be shaped into something new and beautiful. But always there was ballet pulling her away from the rock-garden.

"Am I being horrible to you, Brian?" she asked wistfully one day, as they drove together to the Abbey for a few hours with Rachel. "I don't believe I'm satisfying you. But it's only for a little while and only in my top layers; underneath I'm yours, truly I am."

"That's all I want, my Pirouette," he told her.

"If I could be sure of it!" he said to himself, when they were back in town and he saw her absorbed and happy in her work again. "She means what she says, but does she know herself?"

And Rachel and he shared a secret anxiety all through the autumn and winter.

Rachel was not lonely, though she was alone in the Abbey. The twins and Rosemary, and even Jansy, came to beg for instalments of their "secret serial," as Jansy called it; and Myonie Manley spent many Saturdays at the Manor and was always eager for stories. Her mother and baby brother were well, and Clover was much cheered by the friendship which surrounded her, and particularly by the companionship which Rosamund gave her at this time. The car fetched her and the baby to Kentisbury continually, and Rosamund delighted in little John, and watched Clover, as she fed and tended him, with wistful eyes.

"Our crowd are getting so big!" she said. "Even the tinies will be three in May. It seems a long while since we had a real little one in the Castle!"

Queen Lavender came to the Abbey too, to report on progress at school. "Tessa's as different as she can be, and everybody likes her much better," she said. "She's still good fun, but she doesn't do lunatic tricks any more. We're all much relieved!"

"I'm sure you are. Do you think she'll be the next Queen?"

"I know she will," Rosalind said simply.

"Good! The Club would be grateful to you, if they understood."

"They mustn't understand. But they'll be satisfied, and that's all that matters."

In her spare time—and she had many spare hours during the winter—Rachel was writing the school story Mary had suggested, and was surprised and amused to find how it had gripped her interest. She was enjoying the work more than she had done the writing of her novel, about which, she confessed to Mary-Dorothy, she had always been a little nervous.

"Perhaps it wasn't quite convincing enough,"

Mary agreed. "You're happier in this book for girls?"

"Oh, this is fun! I can hardly bear to leave it!"

"Good!" Mary laughed. "That's how you ought to feel."

"It's writing itself. I only put it down on paper."

"It will be a good book," Mary told her.

Christmas brought Damaris home for a few days' quiet and rest, and Rachel told her of the book and allowed her to read the manuscript. Damaris plunged into it and was enthralled at once.

"Ray, this is wonderful! I've always loved your writing; I like this better than anything you've done. It's fun to find these true stories in a book! You've brought our days at Dorothy's to life, for all sorts of girls to read!"

"You don't mind my using our experiences?" Rachel asked. "I felt I ought to let you read it.

"I'm glad. Put me in as a schoolgirl as much as you like."

"I'm afraid I have done just that," Rachel confessed.

"You certainly have!" Damaris grinned. "I recognise lots of me in the story. Go ahead and have it published, Ray! It's a great yarn. What will you call yourself?"

"How do you mean?"

"Rachel Ellerton writes grown-up stuff. Your fame may not be world-wide——"

Rachel laughed. "Ass!"

"But your name must be known fairly well, if only to the agents and editors. You should call yourself something new for this story; it's quite a different sort of work. Lots of people write under more than one name."

"I hadn't thought of using another. I'd rather stick to my own. It won't matter to anyone who reads this that I've done a few grown-up stories."

"No, but it may matter to the next editor who considers one of your ' grown-ups,' that you've done a book for children," Damaris retorted. "If this is a big success and makes your name, as I believe it will, people will look on you as a children's author and they'll be prejudiced against your older stuff. I'm sure you ought to have another name."

"I'll talk it over with Mary-Dorothy, but I don't really see any need for it," Rachel began.

"Ray! Oh, Ray! Call yourself Ray Damayris!" Damaris gave a shout. "I suggested it years ago, but you would stick to Ellerton. Ray Damayris wouldn't be connected with Rachel Ellerton! Oh, Ray! Take over my name and carry it on, when I give it up!"

"I couldn't!" Rachel exclaimed. "It would seem like making capital out of your success. I couldn't trade on your name!"

"Ass! Oh, idiot! I want you to use it!"

Rachel shook her head. "I'll talk to Mary, but I don't like the idea."

"You'll get used to it. When will the book be ready? Will it be out by June?"

"Don't be daft! It may be years before anybody takes it! Why June?"

"I want a copy for a wedding-present."

"Is it to be in June?" Rachel asked, relief in her heart.

"That's the idea. I must give Madame and Antoine their three months, and I'm only to start in March. You think I'm going to let Brian down, don't you? Well, I'm not. I keep telling him he needn't look so frightened. I know what he thinks."

"It's only because he knows how much you love your dancing."

"Can't I love him more? If he will worry, he'll have to put up with it. I'll show him, one day. Give me some more story, and go away and leave me in peace with it!"

Rachel said no more and hoped all would be well. But the test of the public performance was still to come. Would Damaris really be strong enough to turn from her career, if Mary Damayris had a great triumph?

The girls were alone in the Abbey, except for Rory and Mrs. Nigger, for Benedicta was spending Christmas with Gail and Jim and Penny Rose. Rosalind was with her married sister and baby niece, and Jansy had gone home to her parents and her brothers and sisters. There were family parties at the Hall and the Manor, so for a few days Rachel was not required to supply chapters of a secret serial, which might become a book some day.

There was no party at the Castle, but Clover Manley and Hermione and the baby were invited to stay for a week and went joyfully to join the family.

"We're a party in ourselves, without outsiders," Rosamund laughed. "With Roddy and Hugh and four small girls we do very well. Myonie Rose can play with our crowd, and Clover and I will take care of little John. I like to ask a lot of people here, but for this year we can do with a quiet Christmas."

Contrary to their usual habits, the Hamlet Club held a party in the Abbey barn soon after the spring term began, and Tessa was invited to be the next Queen.

"It's very early to talk of it," said Jansy, who made the announcement. "But we've quite decided, so you may as well know. We want you and we don't want anyone else, Theresa."

In a moment Tessa was up on a chair, vainly trying to make herself heard. When the cheering had died down she said vehemently, "Not if you call me Theresa! I simply can't bear it. Thank you very much, all of you! I'd love to be Queen, and I'll try to be about half as good as Lavender has been, which is the most I can promise. But only if I can be Queen Tessa. I will not go up on the school walls for ever as Queen Theresa!"

"It's a very good name." Rosalind laughed at her. "It sounds most royal and stately. Couldn't you get used to it?"

"I could not! It doesn't sound like me at all.

Please, Lavender—and everybody! I should hate it. It would spoil the whole year for me!"

"I tried to make them call me Queen Janice, but they never remembered," Jansy said mournfully.

"You were such a spot when you were Queen; we couldn't think of you as Janice. Now that you're so much taller we could start, if you like," said Phyl, Tessa's friend and—as she knew very well—her future Maid of Honour.

"Don't trouble," Jansy said haughtily. "It's not worth while now. We'll call Tessa what she likes best. I've been told that when Aunty Jen was chosen she said she wouldn't go, if they tried to turn her into Queen Janet. Three cheers for Queen Tessa, Hamlet Clubbers!"

CHAPTER XXVIII

A RING FOR RACHEL

On Sunday afternoon, after the choosing party in the barn, Jen wandered into the Abbey for a chat with the Guardian.

Nobody was to be seen, but the parlour and workroom doors were unlocked, so she knew Rachel had not gone for a walk.

Jen stood on the garth and piped a few notes of "We won't go Home till Morning," which had closed the party the night before. Then she waited expectantly.

In the sacristy, out of sight of the garth, Rachel raised her head in surprise. Then she came quickly to the gap in the wall which led to the site of the great church.

"Lady Jen! Mrs. Brown! How nice of you to come!"

"I like 'Mrs. Brown' best," Jen told her. "What were you doing? Dreaming over the font?"

"Something like that. I was sitting in the rose window."

"We'll both sit in the rose window, as Joy used to do. Your cats welcomed me—at least, Rory did; he came to speak to me very courteously. But he couldn't tell me where to find you."

"Your pipe is as good as a trumpet call." Rachel led the way back to the sacristy. "Have one of my cushions! I brought two, but one is enough."

Jen seated herself on the broken window-ledge on a blue cushion. "Were you feeling lonely? No Dammy-Marry this week-end?"

"She's gone to Brian's people to-day. She's always happy with them."

"And no schoolgirls? Rosemary told me the last secret serial was finished."

Rachel laughed. "I've demanded a rest. I can't spin out serials without a break. Even Jansy and the twins admitted I must have a week or two to think up some new people."

"You are good to those girls! They all love you. Their families are very grateful to you."

"They needn't be. I love to have them here. They tell me things about school, and they're delighted if I work some of them into stories."

"I'm sure they are! I wish I'd had their chances! Do you think our new Queen will do well? I saw you dancing with Lavender last night."

"Lavender asked me. I appreciated the honour of a dance with the reigning Queen! Oh, yes! Tessa should do very well."

"Were you surprised when she was chosen?"

"No, Mrs. Brown."

Jen gave her a quick look. "You knew?"

"It isn't all fun being trusted with other people's secrets!" Rachel broke out. "It's rather like the confessional. When I'm told things I'm expected to keep them to myself. I don't like it!"

"That's really very interesting!" Jen exclaimed. "The Abbot must keep the secrets trusted to him; yes, I see! Whose idea was that?"

"Several people. I'm not allowed to pass on the things I'm told."

"And so they feel they can trust you. My dear, you're even more valuable than I thought! I won't ask questions, but I am very much intrigued!"

"I don't suppose it matters now that Tessa is Queen-elect. I knew last autumn that she would be chosen—and that she would wear lupin colours."

"You did?" Jen cried. "You kept that secret well! I suppose you talked it over with Rosalind?"

"Rosalind talked it over with me! I can't say any more, but you can ask her, if you like. She did a good bit of work for the Hamlet Club. Somebody ought to know. I daresay she would tell you now."

"She has done more than one good turn for the Club! And for other people too; her coming to the school was a very happy thing. I'm deeply grateful to her for Rosemary's sake; and so are Myonie and her mother. I wish we could keep Rosalind for another year, but her Cookery course will be over in March. We don't want to lose her."

"What about her music? Could she live here and go on studying in Oxford or London? She ought to have the very best, and Lady Virginia's home is right in the country, isn't it?"

"I believe so. There might be something in that idea," Jen said hopefully. "I know Rosalind means to live with her sister, but perhaps she could come to one of us for short spells, a few weeks at a time and work up her music with a first-class master. I believe she'd be glad not to say good-bye to Jansy and the rest."

"And she'd like to watch Tessa as Queen."

"I'm sure she would. But I must tell you why I came to see you, Abbey Lady."

Rachel raised her brows. "Was there a reason? I hoped you just came. Just to see me, you know."

"I did. But I had something rather special to say. Do you know what this is?"

Rachel looked with interest at a wide gold ring, which Jen had taken from her finger. "A ring, Mrs. Brown? I haven't seen you wearing it before."

"I don't wear it now. I did, for several years, but when Kenneth gave me an engagement ring and then a wedding ring, and several old family rings, I put the plain gold one away. Look at it carefully, Rachel."

"There are flowers engraved all round it. I believe—are they fleur-de-lis? And roses?"

"They are. You don't know what it is? You've never heard of that ring?"

"I don't think so." Rachel looked puzzled.

"Somebody has been slack; probably me. It's old Ambrose's keepsake ring. Jehane gave him some gold and told him to make a ring and wear it, for her sake; they knew they could never marry, but Ambrose loved her and she understood. He was a worker in gold and jewels, and he engraved the roses and fleur-de-lis all round the ring. He came from France, and the fleur-de-lis used to stand for France; the roses were for Jehane, I suppose."

"And he used to meet her by the gate-house, among roses and lilies!" Rachel added. "What a treasure! Where did you find it?"

"Near his grave, below the gate-house, with the book in which he had written the story of his wanderings after the Abbey was destroyed. He told how Jehane had died and he had come back to the Abbey. But you must have read all that?"

"Oh, yes! But I didn't know the ring had been found. How wonderful to have it! A real link with Ambrose!"

"Joan gave it to me; there were reasons for that. But I always felt it belonged to the Abbey and that it wasn't quite mine. I want it to come back to the Abbey. Would it fit you?"

Dazed, Rachel allowed her to try the ring on her finger. "But, Lady Jen! You couldn't——"

"It fits beautifully. There, Abbey Guardian— your Abbot's ring!"

"I couldn't take it!" Rachel cried. "Oh, I never could! It's far too precious!"

"It's the Abbey ring. I asked Joan last night and she agreed. She'll like to think Ambrose's ring is in the Abbey again."

Rachel drew a long breath. "It would be my

very greatest treasure! But I feel I ought not to take it."

"You'll wear it, won't you?" Jen asked anxiously. "Don't put it away! I want it to be worn. I have too many others now. Wear the Abbey ring all the time, Rachel! It wouldn't have occurred to me to give it to your Aunt Ann; she'd have looked silly wearing a ring! But it looks just right on you. And Aunt Ann never did for the Abbey what you're doing. She was never the Abbot, who helped and advised people and kept their secrets!"

"But you oughtn't to give it to me!" Rachel protested again.

"You told me you had married the Abbey. You ought to have a ring," Jen said. "If you ever decide to marry someone else and go away, you can give it back to me, and I'll give it to your successor—if I like her well enough! But as long as you are our Abbot, I want you to wear the keepsake ring."

"I'll take it as a loan, and I'll try to be worthy of it," Rachel said, deeply moved. "If ever you aren't satisfied, or if you feel I've let you and Ambrose and the Abbey down, you must take the ring back, Mrs. Brown."

"Right! As long as you stay in the Abbey, you'll wear the keepsake ring. I shall be happy to think it's here again. Now I must go home; Jansy and the twins are coming to tea with Rosemary. Good-bye!"

Jen waved her pipe in farewell and left Rachel

standing by the font, looking down at the ring.

"Gloating over it! Nice girl!" Jen said to herself, as she crossed the garth. "I could only have parted with that ring to somebody who would understand!"

She looked back as she reached the tresaunt, and saw Rachel run across the garth to her home within the walls.

"Going to ring up Mary Damayris and tell her all about it," Jen murmured. "Dammy-Marry will be pleased! It will intrigue her that Rachel should have a ring, too. I am glad I thought of it!"

CHAPTER XXIX

HEATHER AND CROCUS

THE BELLS rang gaily in Kentisbury one day in February, and the Abbey clan rejoiced, for Rosamund's second son was born, and she and Geoffrey were very proud and happy.

"He's to be Geoffrey John," she said to Maidlin, always the first to see the babies at the Castle. "Clover is so pleased! But we shall call him Geoff. Roddy's thrilled to have what he calls ' another of those little things '—meaning nephew."

"Another of the ' little children who are too young to understand,' I suppose," Maidlin smiled. "He's a lovely boy, Ros. You have such large beautiful children, just as Jen does. Mine are always so tiny."

"But they soon grow. Your Jackie-Paul is a fine little chap, and Marjory and Dorothy are quite big girls now. Nanny and Hyacinth are so pleased about Geoff! They were afraid they were going to lose their job in a year or two, when our girls are old enough for a nursery governess. A new baby means several years more at Kentisbury for them."

"Isn't Agatha pleased, too?"

"She's leaving us this summer to be married. It's been put off once or twice, but we've found her man a really good job now. We're expecting Queen Lilac to come from college to help us, and in time there will be Queen Jean, too. But she isn't through her course yet."

"Quite a collection of Queens! Is Wild Rose going to be your governess?"

"We've asked her. But it's a long way off and she's enjoying her teaching in Wycombe."

"You won't be able to go to the first performance of *The Goose-girl*," Maidlin remarked.

"No; I'm sorry to miss it. But Geoff is worth it! I shall be ready for the wedding. Is Damaris really going to give it all up in June?"

"She says so. She's going to retire and be a gardener, and wear shorts and work among her rock plants. I hope she'll do it."

As the day for the come-back of Mary Damayris drew near, Brian grew more and more anxious, watching her joyful excitement in an experience in which he had no part, or only the very small one of onlooker. Damaris was intensely happy and sure of herself; was it possible that she could be willing to give up so much for him?

"Have I the right to expect it of her?" he asked himself, again and again. "This has been the greatest thing in her life. How can I hope to give her something greater still?"

When they met Damaris read the question in his face.

"Do you grudge me my three months of dancing?" she demanded. "Isn't it rather hard, when you're going to have all the rest?"

"I want you, Pirouette. But I feel guilty," he said.

"Oh, là, là!" said Damaris. "I can't be in two places at once! And I can't do two things. If I go on dancing, I can't make your garden at Heather Garth!"

"I'm afraid you may not think the garden is worth it."

"If it were only the garden I might not," she jeered. "But aren't you worth it?"

"That's for you to say. Antoine and Bernard look at me most reproachfully. They feel I'm committing a crime in asking you to leave them."

"So you are. You're murdering Mary Damayris and she's been quite a nice girl. But she has nothing to do with rock gardens or being married. The poor thing will have to die. You can't blame Antoine; he's broken-hearted," Damaris said lightly.

She rang up Rachel, the night before the first performance. "You are coming, all of you, aren't you? Good! Oh, I'm all right! Feeling frightfully jolly and fit, and looking forward to it enormously. I say, Ray, I want something! Whose car are you coming in?"

"The Manor car; Sir Ken and Lady Jen are bringing Benedicta and me. Lady Joy and Sir Ivor are bringing Mary-Dorothy and Rosalind and Jansy and the twins, so they wouldn't have room."

"That's what I hoped. Ask Sir Ken if he'll bring me home after the show."

"But, Marry dear, won't you be too tired? He will, of course, but oughtn't you to rest and come to us on Sunday morning, if you can spare a few hours?"

"Yes, I know I ought, but I'm not going to do it. I'm coming home. I've had it out with Madame and made her agree. I can get anything I want out of her just now. It's terribly bad for me! Brian will have to be very stern with me, when he gets me to himself; I'm being thoroughly spoiled! I expect he'll have to beat me a few times, till I settle down. I can manage Madame! I'll come back to town early on Monday; she'll want to tell me off for all my faults and failures. And there's the show at night. But I must have the week-end quietly with you—I must! I want my own bed that night."

"I'd like it better than anything, if it won't be too much for you. But what about Brian, Marry? It's his right to drive you home."

"I don't want him. I shall be too tired to talk, and if he's there I shall want to talk. I've told him to come to the Abbey on Sunday afternoon."

"I see," Rachel said soberly. "It's all right, isn't it, Marry?"

"Do you think I'm going to throw him over?" Damaris jeered.

"What are you going to do?"

"Tell him a few home-truths. But not till I've had a good night's rest. Good-bye!"

"I agree with you about the night's rest," Rachel cried, as they were cut off.

"We'll be proud and honoured to bring the lady home," Kenneth said. "There'll be plenty of room."

"And we won't let her talk," Jen added. "We're taking Rosemary, but she'll probably sleep all the way back. Mary Damayris had better do the same."

"She's more likely to be terribly over-excited," Rachel said. "Last time she didn't sleep for hours."

"She's right to come," Jen decided. "If she stayed in town all her crowd would buzz round and insist on supper-parties, and she'd talk all night. The quiet of the Abbey will soothe her, whether she sleeps or not. She's very wise."

The stalls held a long row of Abbey friends, and John Grant Grandison and his wife sat near them, with Brian. It seemed to Rachel and Jen that he looked white, almost as if he dreaded the performance.

"The more wonderful it is the worse he'll feel, poor chap," Jen murmured.

"I'm afraid so, Mrs. Brown," Rachel agreed. "I'll be glad when it's over."

"And when to-morrow afternoon is over, too," she said to herself. "I don't know what Marry is going to say, but I hope it's something that will ease his mind. He has looked so worried lately!"

Brian came to speak to her before the curtain rose. "Frightened, Sister Rachel?"

"Not really. I know Marry can do it. There's nothing to be upset about." She gave him a look full of meaning.

"You're going to be a proud man to-night," said Jen.

"I feel terribly torn in two, Mrs. Brown." He had adopted the nickname months before. "How is my friend Brownie? Looking forward to the show?"

"She can hardly sit still," Jen told him. "We're all thrilled to the limit."

"And I feel like a criminal."

"Oh, it's not as bad as that! But you're going to take something beautiful out of the world when you run off with Mary Damayris," Jen said severely.

"I know. I've been to rehearsals; I realise what I'm doing. Sometimes I wonder if it's right."

"Oh, tosh!" Jen exclaimed. "She wants to be run off with! Have you seen her this evening?"

"This afternoon, for one moment. She asked me not to bring her flowers, as she'd have far too many, and it was true. She's completely buried in tulips and daffodils. You all sent lovely presents —they made her very happy. But she liked Rachel's crocuses best."

"Some golden ones, from the gate-house," Rachel said, in answer to Jen's look. "I packed them with their stems in moss. They won't last, but I thought Marry might be cheered by the sight of them. It's just two years since Jansy showed her Aunt Ann's clump of crocuses in the corner, and that gave her the idea of the Abbey garden. I knew I couldn't compete with the lovely things you and Lady Kentisbury and the rest would send, but I didn't believe anyone else would think of golden crocuses."

"She knew what you meant," Brian said. "She told me she loved them most of all and they were a message from the Abbey. She's greatly thrilled by a box of roses from Daphne and Dicky Dandy, in New York—sent through a florist here, of course."

"How kind of Daphne to think of it! She was the girl whose life Damaris saved," Rachel said.

"Did you obey the lady and not send anything?" Kenneth asked.

"I took her a bunch of purple heather."

They all looked at him quickly.

"Good for you! You knew what she'd like," Rachel exclaimed.

"Where did you find heather in March?" Kenneth asked.

"Florist. You can get anything, if you go to the right place. There are plenty of winter heaths."

"It was a good thought," Jen said, with approval. "She'd appreciate your meaning."

"She was pleased." Brian smiled. "She said it was another message from home, and that it reminded her of Heather Garth. It looked odd among her hothouse beauties, but she liked it.

The heather and crocuses are in the place of honour in her dressing-room; she says they'll bring her good luck. But I must go. The great moment has come," and he went to his seat.

"Looking a little grim," Jen murmured. "And the bigger her success the worse he'll feel, poor lamb!"

CHAPTER XXX

THE RETURN OF MARY DAMAYRIS

GRANDISON, the composer, smiled as the familiar music began. The villagers danced, the soldiers appeared and drove them away; they shrank to the sides of the stage in frightened groups.

Then came those fateful notes on the flute, and suddenly Damaris was there, in her tattered gown, with wildly-flying hair, the Goose-girl from the hills.

Brian caught his breath. His mother's hand stole out and held his.

But what was this? The whole house rose to greet her, with thunderous applause. She stopped, bewildered, unable to hear the music.

"But I hadn't done anything!" she protested afterwards.

"They greeted you because of your gallant leap to save Daphne and your courage in returning, my child," Madame explained.

"I couldn't think what was wrong with them," Damaris confessed. "I thought they were all crazy."

She looked, indeed, entirely puzzled, and stood, hesitating and doubtful, as the cheers rang through the theatre. Then she bobbed a little curtsy and turned and ran away.

"Make them stop!" She flung herself on Antoine in the wings. "I can't go on. I can't hear a sound. Are they mad?"

"It is a welcome for you, my dear. They will be quiet now," Antoine said. "Shall thank I them for you?"

"Oh, please! I never thought they'd do this!"

Antoine went out and raised his hand. The clapping died away, and he said briefly, "Miss Damayris thanks you for your kind greeting. She asks that the ballet may proceed."

As he withdrew the flute notes came once more, and with heightened colour Damaris ran out, to begin her wild dance with Bernard, the shepherd from the hills.

The curtain fell with the shepherd kneeling by her prostrate body and cursing the foreign king.

"She looks as pathetic as ever," Rachel murmured to Benedicta, who had watched every movement, enraptured. "She always looks such a sad little white thing, lying there! I'm going to speak to Brian; there's just time."

"She's lovely," Benedicta said. "She ought not to give it up."

"Don't say that to Brian! It's how he feels. But he wants her very badly. And she wants him, too."

Rachel made her way to Brian's seat. "Are you proud of your girl?"

"Wonderful girl!" He rose quickly to speak to her. "Rachel, how can I ask her to leave all this?"

Q

"You can, and you must. You'd break her heart, if you didn't. Besides, you have asked her already."

"I didn't realise—that overwhelming welcome —they all love her. It seems a terrible thing—to take her away, just for myself."

"It's quite as much for her sake. She'll be happier, you know. If I hadn't been sure of that I'd have tried to discourage her. She really will have a happier life. I'll have to go. But don't forget! She'll be happier with you." And Rachel slipped away.

Breathless, Brian watched the sad little solo dance in the king's garden. Damaris was a slave now, neatly dressed in a short white tunic, with a fillet binding her hair, and her dance was tamed and more finished. He watched the drama to its happy ending; saw her famous dance before the king, saw her *pas de deux* with Bernard, saw her kneel to be crowned and dismissed with her shepherd-lover to rule over her own people.

Then the curtain fell once more, and the house rang with shouts of "Damayris! We want Damayris!"

Time after time she came out to bow, with the whole company, with Bernard, with Antoine. Flowers were handed to her, to add to those already heaped in her dressing-room; over a huge bunch of daffodils she looked down into the stalls and smiled at Brian.

At what she saw in his face and in the smile he gave her, she waved her hand to the crowd and fled to her room. Madame, hurrying in, found her scribbling a line on a scrap of paper, her flowers flung aside.

"My child, you have done well. But you must change quickly, if you are to be our Fairy. You are sure it is not too much? You wished it so greatly."

"Not a scrap too much. I want to be Fairy; it will be a relief. That Goose-girl always works me up." Damaris signed her name, folded the note round a sprig of heather and gave it to Madame. "Oh, please, Madame! Ask somebody—Antoine himself—to give this to Brian. I can't dance again till he's read it. I'll change at full speed."

Madame took the note, and Damaris gave herself into her dresser's hands, to be transformed into the teasing Fairy in the rainbow gown, her curls tucked out of sight in a dark hood. Under the gay skirt was the white tarlatan in which she would appear in the wood, in the second little scene. It had been her great wish that for this first night the programme should include *Rainbow Corner* as well as *The Goose-girl*, and she had insisted that it would not be too much; but ordinarily only one of her ballets would be given at each performance.

Brian smiled at the heather and read the note.

"' *Don't* look like that! You break my heart. I'm all yours. Please look happy! Dammy.'"

He put the note away, his face still sober. "Then she saw, although I smiled at her. ' All mine! ' Not quite. These others claim their share. ' We want Damayris! ' So do I!"

As Damaris had insisted would be the case, the little story of the distressed Widow and the Wicked Fairy came as a relief, after the drama of *The Goose-girl*. There was laughter as well as applause, as Damaris mocked the Widow with her gift of gold and her demand that her name should be guessed or the baby be given to her; and more laughter as she danced exultantly in the wood, a slim white whirling sprite, while Irina Ivanovna, the tall Widow, hid behind a tree and learned the secret name. But while the people laughed, they revelled in the beauty of the woodland dance and in the thrill of the last scene in the cottage, when the Fairy mocked the Widow again, and then, when the name was guessed, danced wildly off the stage in a rage.

"Oh, bravo! Well danced! Well done!" came from every corner of the house.

"Mon Dieu, she was right!" Madame murmured. "It makes a good finish. We looked on it as too slight, a mere interlude between serious work. But it closes the evening on a merry note and everyone goes home happy and content. She is an artist, Damayris, and she knew!"

Rosalind Kane looked down at Jansy Raymond, who was very quiet. "Didn't you like it, Lob? See how thrilled the twins are!"

"They didn't see that other time." Jansy explained herself with difficulty. "I can't forget it. I keep expecting something from up there to come down and kill her."

"Oh, but it won't happen again! You needn't worry over her."

"I know. I'm not worried. But I can't forget that other night. She's lovely, isn't she, Nanta Rose?"

"Quite perfect. I'm to tell Aunt Rosamund all about it, as she can't be here."

"And I'm going to write to Marigold. She saw it happen, that other time. She'd have loved to be here to-night with us," Jansy said wistfully.

Kenneth came to Rachel. "You know the back premises of these places. Can you get hold of the lady and ask her to be quick? We want to take Brownie home to bed. She's half asleep."

"I'm not! Father, I'm not! It was lovely!"

"It was," Jen agreed, as Rachel went off. "But it's long past your bedtime, my lass. Think what a lot you have to tell Myonie on Monday!"

Rachel made her way into the seething excitement back-stage. She heard her sister's voice before she reached her.

"Clear out, everyone, and let me get dressed! I'll see you all on Monday; I'm off for a week-end in the country. Somebody see to my flowers; they'll be all right in water. I'll take Daphne's roses with me, and the daffodils from the Manor, and the heather, and those crocuses. And those white narcissus; they're from Maidlin; and the gorgeous tulips from Kentisbury. The rest must wait for me—unless you'd send some of them to hospitals, Madame? I wish you would. There are far too many. Oh, here's my Guardian-Angel! All right, Ray. I'm almost ready."

"Sir Ken's getting restive." Rachel made her way through the crowd, who were still trying to give congratulations. "Can I help?"

"You can take those roses and daffodils. I'll carry the heather and your crocuses myself. I loved them; they must go back to the Abbey. There, that's everything! Am I clean? I must be decent to face Lady Jen."

"You look all right. I'll carry your flowers."

"Were you proud, Sister-Mother?" asked Madame.

"Very proud, and most grateful to you, Madame. It made us all very happy to see Mary Damayris again. There's just one day that will make me happier still."

"Her wedding day. C'est-ça!" Madame agreed. "Good-night, my child! Rest well, and come to us on Monday!"

"I'm sorry to leave the other flowers behind. I'd have liked you to see them, Mrs. Brown. But I've brought your glorious daffodils, and Maid's narcissus, and the Kentisbury tulips," Damaris said, as she tumbled into a corner of the car and lay still. "If I'd brought the lot we'd have needed a special cart, to follow us, like at a funeral."

Kenneth grinned. "What a picture, Mary Damayris!"

"Mary Damayris is very much alive. You were wonderful, Dammy-Marry," Jen told her. "You gave us a very great treat."

"All the same, she's going to have a funeral soon. There's no hope for the poor girl," Damaris said. "Oh, gosh! I'm tired! Do you mind if I go to sleep?"

"Follow Rosemary's good example," Rachel suggested. "She's dropping off already."

"It was huge fun," Damaris murmured wearily. "I loved every minute of it. But somehow I'm just terribly glad to get away and come home quietly with you dear people. I'd had about enough. I've a sort of feeling—but I'll tell you later." She lapsed into silence, and presently they saw she was asleep.

CHAPTER XXXI

PLANS FOR A WEDDING

THE ABBEY was very quiet. Rachel was irresistibly reminded of their first night as the Guardians.

Benedicta was left at her cottage in the village. The car raced on to the Manor, with Rosemary sleeping soundly in her mother's arms.

Damaris, roused by Rachel's insistent, "Wake up, Marry dear! We're home," stumbled through the gate-house and up the gravel drive, still half asleep, but clinging to her heather and crocuses. "How nice the sweet-briar smells!" She paused. "And isn't it peaceful? I am glad you brought me home."

Rachel, her arms full of daffodils and roses, had difficulty in unlocking the gate. "There! I didn't drop one rose-bud. Come and rest, Marry; the fire will soon burn up. I'll get supper in five minutes."

"I'm rested now; I'll help. I had a lovely sleep in the car."

"You did, but you won't help. Sit by the fire and keep out of my way. I'll put these beautiful things in water. Here are Rory and Mrs. Nigger, glad to see us back."

The cats rose as they came in, Rory with his

usual grave courtesy, Mrs. Nigger skipping to meet them as if she was still a kitten.

"Glad to see you, children!" and Damaris sank into a big chair and lay looking at the fire, which Rachel was coaxing into a flame. The cats leapt upon her, and she stroked them gently and set them singing.

"Was it all right, Ray? You're a stern critic."

"Better than ever! You had a wonderful welcome."

"Wasn't it marvellous? I thought they'd all gone mad. I nearly wept. They really do like me!"

"Did you doubt it?" Rachel smiled down at her, as she picked up the flowers from the table.

"I didn't know they'd feel like that about my going back. I was thunderstruck. I ran away to ask Antoine what they meant."

"How lovely Daphne's roses are!" and Rachel arranged them in a big bowl. "It was a beautiful thought."

Damaris watched her hands, as she touched the flowers gently. "Your wonderful ring! I love to see you wearing it, Abbot!"

"I love to wear it. Everybody has congratulated me. I'm very proud of it," Rachel said quietly. "Now won't you go to bed and have supper there?"

"That's an idea." Damaris rose wearily. "I love supper in bed after a show. Sir Ken's chocolates and Lady Jen's coffee and sandwiches saved my life in the car, but I'm hungry again, now."

"Get into bed!" Rachel commanded. "After supper I shall massage you, as I used to do, and you can have a hot bath."

She put the bowl of roses on the table by the bed and a tall jar of daffodils on the window-sill, and Damaris lay and looked at them happily.

"My heather and crocuses on the small table, close to me, Ray," she begged. "There, that's nice! A thousand times better than a noisy party in town!"

"You really mean that?" Rachel paused on her way to the kitchen. "You wouldn't always have said it."

"I do mean it. I want just you. And Brian, of course; but I'll have him to-morrow."

Rachel brought a light supper, an omelette, fruit and cake, and coffee. "The grapes came from Kentisbury, with a note saying they were for you to-night and an apology because there weren't any strawberries."

Damaris laughed. "How like our dear Countess! She was thinking of my first show, when she sent strawberries and you had to keep me from making myself ill. Fancy her remembering that!"

"Do you feel better?" Rachel asked presently, after the hot bath and the massage she had suggested, a note of mock anxiety in her voice. "Do you feel strong?"

"Ray! What's up? There's meaning in your eye! What has happened?"

"History is repeating itself. I had a letter this morning——"

"Your book!" Damaris shouted. "Tell me, Ray!"

"You terrified Mrs. Nigger with that yell. They like it, and they hope to publish it in the autumn, if we can come to terms."

"Oh, cheers! Cheers by the thousand! You'll have a book of your own at last! And what's your name, Ray? You are going to use mine, I hope?"

Rachel coloured. "Mary-Dorothy advised it; she agreed with you that a new name would be wise, and she said it would be a compliment to use yours, so I put Rachel Damayris."

"It's a jolly good name! I am bucked! Damayris won't be forgotten, after all. I'm proud, Ray! Thank you for the compliment; Mary-Dorothy is right about that. Do you wish it had been the novel?"

"No, I like this new work. The novel may find a home soon."

"Aren't the school crowd fearfully pleased? They heard it told to them first."

"They don't know yet. No one knows but Mary-Dorothy. You had to hear before anybody. I'll tell them to-morrow."

"How jolly nice of you! Rachel Damayris! I like it better than Ray, as I suggested."

"Ray isn't a name. And anyway, it belongs to you. It's not for the general public."

"I want to tell you something, Ray—two things!" Damaris lay stroking Mrs. Nigger, while Rory tramped on the bed and then went singing noisily to have his ears pulled by Rachel.

She fondled him gently. "I want to hear, Marry."

"It was because of Brian I was so happy to-night —because he was there, in the back of my mind. I wouldn't be satisfied without him. It was tremendous fun and I loved every minute of it, but it wouldn't be enough—not to go on doing it all my life. I want something more."

"And the something is Brian. You've grown, Marry dear. Two years ago a triumph like to-night's would have satisfied you completely."

"It wouldn't do it now. I'm glad I've danced again; I'm sure I was right. But I'll be ready to give it up and go to Brian when the time comes."

"You'll tell him to-morrow? He doesn't doubt your love for him, but he feels he is taking a beautiful thing out of the world by asking you to give up dancing, and he isn't easy in his mind."

"Am I a thing?" Damaris mocked.

"Not you; your dancing. He feels guilty, but he wants you."

"He's going to have me. Can I be married here, Ray? That's the second thing I want to say. I must be married from the Abbey."

"Of course you must," Rachel agreed. "We'll ring the bells for your wedding. Maidlin and Mrs. Joan, and Lady Joy and Lady Jen, were all married in our village church."

"The Kentisbury wedding was there, too. I want to be like all the rest of them. Madame's very much upset; she wants me to have a big show in town, as Daphne did, and an enormous reception. But I don't want it, and neither does Brian."

"I'm sure Brian would choose a village wedding! Anyone in town who cares enough can come to the church, and I expect the Manor and the Hall will fight for the honour of giving a reception for you."

"I'll give my vote to Lady Jen, because she's our Mrs. Brown. I'll tell Brian it's all planned, and Madame and the rest will have to put up with it. I'm glad that's settled! I want Michael and Cecily to ring for me!"

"Now you've an easy mind about it, go to sleep!" Rachel commanded, and she removed the cats and left her to be quiet and to sleep, if she could.

Brian's car drew up at the Abbey gate next day and he sprang out, to find his lady sitting on the wall, clad in shorts and a jersey, with uncovered hair blowing in the wind.

"Do I look like a famous dancer?" she demanded. "I'm trying to look like a girl who is going to make a rock-garden and take care of a lavender farm."

Brian stood over her and looked down at her. "Is it true, Pirouette? Is it possible? After last night, can you bear it?"

"I'm glad to have had last night," Damaris said dreamily. "I'd never have known, if I hadn't danced again."

"Known what?" he demanded, his tone sharp with fear.

Damaris glanced up at him. "That you matter to me more than dancing; much more! I might always have wondered how much I really cared. I'd have felt I'd been afraid to dance again, for fear it would take me away from you. I know now, for sure and certain, that you come first. All through the fun last night you were there, in my mind. It was because I have you that I enjoyed it so much; you're something bigger than all that shouting crowd. And when I've played the game by Madame and Antoine, and given them their three months' season, I'll be ready to turn my back on it all and come to you. I shall be looking forward to June."

"Come into the Abbey!" Brian said breathlessly. "I can't say all I want to say out here on the public road!"

Damaris slid from the wall. "Come and tell Rachel we want a quiet corner!"

Rachel heard with laughing eyes. "Go and bury yourselves in the sacristy with the font. That's completely private. And then come and dress yourself, Marry. You look a perfect sight!"

"She looks my own Pirouette," Brian said, and they took hands and raced across the garth together.

THE END